CRUXIM

Book I in the DARK GUARDIAN Trilogy

by

Karin Cox

First published 2012 by Indelible Ink Press
Copyright © Karin Cox 2012
ISBN 978-0-9873602-3-6
Cover Design by Eden Crane Design
Edited by Jessica Meigs

Discover other titles by Karin Cox at http://www.karincox.com and follow her on twitter
@Authorandeditor, Facebook www.facebook.KarinCox.Author or her blog http://www.
karincox.wordpress.com. To become a fan and get advance notice of new releases and
special offers on her title, sign up at http://eepurl.com/vk_bP

CRUXIM

Dedicated to Helen,
for everything.

ONE

It is wet beyond, wet and slippery, but the slight partition I have laboriously scratched out in the wall over decades is still there. My trembling fingers feel for it, seeking the familiar dull sharpness, the blade of cold stone made smooth with scraping—the weapon of my slow-growing hope. I take it out and pry a wedge of stone from the wall to resume my work. Grasping the blunter end and covering my fingers with the twill of my coat, I watch as chips of stone flick up from the blade.

A sparrow is singing. Its cheery trill echoes through the chamber, but I cannot see it. The gray walls outside conceal its plump body. Perhaps it is secreted behind a turret or piling twigs into a crack in the masonry. The pungent odor of the guano that concretes the window mingles with the stench of my sweat from countless nightmares.

Yes, even I have fears.

I scan again, craning my neck through the grate, sliding it with a metallic rattle, but it is the same: slow-growing green lichen mottling the walls, a rust-red trail of water dripping with melancholy repetition from a window ledge.

I am thirsty, or perhaps my throat is dry with anticipation. Maybe tomorrow I will break through to daylight. Today, I smell the sunshine like victory, and I can almost taste my freedom. It swims in my mouth like wine.

It has been more than forty years now. Forty years of solitude, but for the man and then, more recently, the girl, the trembling girl, I assume is his daughter. It would seem a long time to anyone but me. Yet the assault on my liberty bothers me more than the time. It keeps me from my purpose, and my task daily grows larger. When you have lived for centuries, half of a mortal lifespan is a pittance.

The girl comes once a week. Fearful. Fast. She brings me bread, a little thin soup, and sometimes cheese. Very occasionally, a bucket to wash in. She rarely brings meat (I must catch rats and sparrows for that), and never blood. The latter is fine with me. It is not human blood I seek, although they will not believe that. They see the alabaster of my teeth, the high arch of my brow, the silkiness of my dark hair, the gleam of my skin and eyes, and before my incarceration and slow decay, my superhuman strength and speed, and they assume I am one of them. It has ever been thus.

I have given up trying to convince them that I have more in common with man than with those merchants of death: the bloodsucking agents of hell they so fear. I have given up wondering how they could mistake me so, for I am neither demon nor devil. My work is holy.

A gentle breeze cools me, and I realize I am flapping in agitation. Or is it anticipation? I am unsure. My wings are weak now. The tower is cramped, and the cold walls and low ceiling restrict my movement. I wonder if my wings will have the strength to carry my weight, even if I can worm through the crevice I have spent decades scratching out. I look over my shoulder and give my wings a firm flap, noting, with a certain weariness, how dirty, how tatty my once snow-white feathers have become. Some are missing, others blackened, and some are still growing back; yet others I pulled out with my own hands and piled in the corner to create a nest on the frigid stone. Few human comforts are afforded me, and no human rights. It seems I do not deserve a blanket, although I feel the cold. Bitterly.

They did not intend to imprison me, of course. First, they tried to kill me. They tried in every conceivable way. "Torture" you might call it, had it been inflicted on a mortal. They bound me. They slit my throat. They punctured my heart. They drew out my teeth with pliers. They set me alight. They plucked and cauterized my wings. They carved a crucifix into my chest. Still I prevailed. I agonized, I scarred, but I prevailed. They threw holy water on me, read scripture to me, smeared garlic upon me. They left me in sunlight, showed me my own mutilated face in the mirror, placed a silver crucifix around my neck (those poor, misguided men of the cloth). They even tried to exorcise me. Had I any devil in me, it surely would have fled at their ministrations. But I do not.

"You are in concert with Satan. Admit it and we will let you live," they insisted, as if they had the power to do otherwise.

To my knowledge, only two things can kill me, and my captors are unlikely to attempt either.

"I am innocent of such a charge," I protested.

"Liar! Demon! We found you with them."

That much was true. I had been in Paris at the time and had flown out to feed. They had found me with a coven near the village of Sezanne. I was the only awake creature among them; the others hung from the ceiling, tick-full from a night of nourishing themselves on mortal blood. I was perusing the menu, wondering which to take first, when the firebomb burst through the door, closely followed by men with pitchforks. I had not fed for many weeks. I was weak. They caught me off guard. Not so much the men, but the Vampires.

That was only the second time Vampires ever got the better of me. My strength, stealth, and speed usually work to their detriment, but on that occasion I was beset on both sides. All my long life I have fallen somewhere between these two beasts—man and Vampire—and yet I am neither, just as I am neither devil nor truly angel. I am a hybrid, very rare, seldom seen, so little known that some think me nothing more than a chimera. But I am real. I am Cruxim.

The chink of a key in a lock startles me. The girl is coming. I am surprised; it has been less than a week by my reckoning. I cough to muffle the grinding of the stone sliding back into place and hurriedly push the knife back into its nook, wondering, as I do so, why she is here. What change in fortune is afoot to bring this shivering child before me twice in such a short span of time?

It is not that I need the food. I can survive years, decades even, without it, growing weaker but never succumbing. It is that even her small scrap of company is something. Her father (or the man I assume was such) never spoke to me, but sometimes she does. Just a word—"Here"—as she pushes the food through the small door in the bars. Sometimes, she speaks to herself, her lips moving in a prayer that might be for me or, more likely, calls for her God to save her from me.

I suppose I should be grateful for food. At first, the good people of Sezanne tried starving me. They left me for months. When they returned, my eyes burned hatred at them from my wan, thin-skinned face, but I was otherwise unchanged. They left me again. A year this time. My eye sockets ringed my sunken eyes. My ribs were a bony corset in my chest. But I was still alive. Only the return of my wings convinced them to start feeding me again, however infrequently. After all, wings are the guise of the angels. Some count me among them, but I have no recollection of my Maker. All I know is my purpose.

"Here." Today is one of the days she speaks.

I hurry to the bars. "Thank you." Nodding, I stretch a hand out to the pail. It is soup, thin and gray, along with a hunk of bitter bread.

She draws back, one step, two—beyond the reach of even the longest arm.

"Beef?"

She nods, and then, "Yes."

"Tell me. The man who used to come, your father—"

"Uncle."

"What happened to him?"

She looks wary, young. One milk-white hand flies to her hair and she halts indecisively.

"What happened?" I press again.

"He is dead."

Something in me shudders. I know, without her even telling me, that it was them. My fists clench at my sides and I drop my bread to the floor. I can feel the increased heat of her, her fear at my eyes' reddish glow.

"I could do something about this. About them," I snarl. "If only you would let me out." I rattle the bars.

She turns, too quickly, as if she has tarried too long. The white swan of her neck stretches eagerly toward the door out of the tower.

How beautiful it is, I think. How beautiful that slim, graceful neck would be to them. A small silver cross glistens at the hollow of her throat.

At the top of the stairs, she pauses. Head cocked, she looks at me with eyes bluer than lapis, and her lips move again in a silent prayer. There is something wistful in her eyes, sad even. In that moment, she reminds me of Sabine.

TWO

Sabine. How I miss her. I wonder where she is now. Probably perched on a turret or sitting stone-like somewhere, waiting. If only I could let her know where I am. Has she been waiting for me these forty years? Possibly. Her kind are renowned for their patience.

We met more than a century ago, she and I. I had been feeding, had already drank my fill really. The Vampire that lay before me had convulsed into death and his rich blood had already satiated me when I heard a sound unmistakable to a being such as I: the gentle swoosh of wings overhead. Owl-like, I froze.

Recognizing the wing beats, I stared around me for what I thought must be Seraph or Cruxim like myself, and then I saw her.

She, too, had frozen stone-still. For a moment, I thought she was indeed a statue. Only the dull rhythm of her heart, echoing in my ears, and the subtle tic of her tail gave her away.

She was magnificent—is magnificent. Like me, she

knows not the ravages of time. A face so finely wrought it is understandable that many mistake her for sculpture. When she knew I had seen her, she sprang lightly down from the façade behind me with feline grace.

Sabine had been wary, as had I. She had prowled the shadows at first, a low growl issuing from her throat until she finally fixed me with a stare from her jade eyes and said, "You are Cruxim?"

"Yes."

I was enchanted by her, too. By the dusky wings held rigidly away from her body, ready to bear her away until she could be certain of my intentions; by the beauty of her fine-boned face; the perfection of her breasts; but mostly by the supple slinkiness of her lioness body. "And you?" I asked, already anticipating the answer.

It came in a throaty purr. "Sphinx."

"The guardian?"

"Yes."

"You have abandoned your post."

"My charge is dead." She moved forward gracefully and her claws clacked on the cobbles. "Finished?" She nodded towards the corpse that lay before us. Curls, fair and leonine, tumbled around her exquisite face.

"Yes."

"May I?" She nodded at the body again, and I noticed that, although her head was womanly, her teeth were feline. It had never occurred to me that she might need meat.

I was fascinated and smiled at the thought, cruelly you might think. "Go ahead."

She ate hungrily but fastidiously, tearing great strips of meat off, ignoring my stare. All the while, her tail made a slow, snakelike twitching from side to side.

"Aren't your charges always dead?" I asked her, returning to our former conversation in an effort to put her at ease.

She swallowed a mouthful of gristle and placed one

enormous paw on a shoulder socket, tearing up another strip of flesh. Blood coursed over her breasts, which were bare and beguiling where their soft whiteness met the tawny texture of her fur. It was all I could do not to stare.

"Not always," she said. "Mostly."

"You were guarding the undead?" I had been curious, and I overstepped my mark.

"Never!" Her eyes burned, and the stirrings of a roar sprang from her throat.

"Human?"

She nodded again. Her tail twitched faster.

"What is your name?"

"Sabine."

"Amedeo."

"Amedeo the Cruxim," she said, bemused. "I have never met one before."

"Nor I a Sphinx," I told her. "It is hard to say who is rarer."

She had laughed at that, a mellifluous sound, both feminine and fierce. "Yes," she said. "Two curiosities drawn together to feed on the undead."

I squatted in the shadows, reducing my height to her level. "Have you always fed on them?"

"No." She turned her eyes to mine. "Only when I can."

I wondered whether she might disallow my next question, and I paused momentarily. "So you eat humans?"

She fixed me with a stare that was weary but not accusatory. Then she shook her head, making her golden curls bounce. "Deer, sometimes dogs, birds, rabbits and rats at a pinch. Vampires when I can. I rarely have the strength to kill them myself; only you have that pleasure, I believe."

"Indeed." I gestured to the corpse. "Enjoy it, then. Killing them is always my pleasure." Even as I had said it, my thoughts had flown to the one among them I would give anything to never have to kill: Joslyn.

Holed up here in the tower, I have thought about Joslyn

almost as much as Sabine, perhaps more. It is hard to say.

She was just a child when I met her, or rather, when she saw me. I had been shopping in the labyrinthine streets of the Gothic Quarter. My wings were carefully concealed beneath a long black cloak, a style fashionable in Barcelona at the time, and my arms were full of parcels. Just as I made my way from Plaça del Pi back onto La Rambla, a carriage careened around the corner toward me. The horses had taken the bit and screamed and whinnied as they clattered over the stones.

I had long learned, by then, that any injury to my person had the ability to reveal my wings, not to mention my immortality should a physician be called. Avoiding injury was a must. Yet the horses galloped on so quickly, and I was so unprepared—my arms full of bundles and my speed hindered by my heeled leather boots and cape—that, even with my speed, I had little recourse but to do what I did. Turning sideways, I leaped, and without thinking, gave my wings a hearty beat beneath the cloak, trusting them to lift me away from the pounding hooves. It was only when I landed that I saw her.

She had just turned four at the time and was rosy and brown from days spent in the Spanish sun. Azure eyes framed by long, dark lashes gazed at me intently. Then she had smiled, revealing dimples. "Angel," she'd said, pointing.

I realized that not only had she seen me fly a little, but my rapid movement had disturbed my cloak, which lay flung back over one shoulder, exposing the downy white of my wings.

I fixed her with a stare and immediately righted my clothing, settling my wing feathers back flat against my shoulders.

"*El meu angel de la guarda.*" She pointed again insistently, and her face shone.

"No," I answered in my poor Catalan. "No, not your guardian angel. *Jo sóc només un home.* I'm just a man. Man," I said, slapping myself on the chest.

"*Angel de la guarda,*" she repeated defiantly and held her little hands out wide, wanting to be picked up. I shook my head. "No," I repeated, noting that her arms were scarred with burns.

"Joslyn!" A swarthy man hurried out of a nearby house and grabbed her arm, reefing it cruelly toward him. "Come along. There's work to be done."

"No." She wriggled free of his grasp and stepped out toward me.

"Child!" The man grabbed her again. "You will obey your master!"

"No!" Again she twisted from his grasp.

He was impeded by bundles of laundry cast over his shoulder, and he grabbed at her but missed. Kicking out, his foot connected with her shin, and the child cried in pain and struggled free again.

"Joslyn!" He struck out again, kicking her hard in the back as she fled. His capped leather boot met with the lowest point of her spine, and the child fell, face first and writhing in agony on the cobbles. The man wasted no time. Hauling her limp body up, he struck her full force across the face. The child's head snapped back, and tears streamed from those bluer-than-blue eyes.

I could take no more. Darting forward, I picked the man up and threw him backwards against the wall of a church behind. In my anger, I underestimated my own strength; his head hit the stone with a resounding crack and blood showered the stone before he had even slid to the ground.

The girl, Joslyn, had looked at me quizzically for a minute, and then she held out her slim arms again. "*El meu angel de la guarda,*" she repeated, satisfied that it was indeed true.

I took the child to Montgat, to the home of Maria del Santos, my seamstress and as kind a foster mother as Joslyn could hope for. The entire journey, the child stared at me with those eyes, stared and smiled. Senyora del Santos was in her mid fifties and had always wanted a child; as a result, she asked few questions. Those she did ask, I answered with the insistence that the child was mine, illegitimately begotten and now orphaned by her consumptive mother's death. Money had a way of closing lips back then in Catalonia, and it is no different in most places today. I paid Maria a handsome allowance to keep the child, and in some show of guilt or obligation, I visited twice monthly at first.

Soon, I came to look forward to my visits. I would arrive with trinkets: a kitten she named "Velvet," a colorful East Indian parrot in a gilt cage, all manner of dolls, musical instruments, and clothes. The child was excitable and loving and, I learned, was indeed an orphan. Her mother had been a slave in the dead man's laundry. When her mama had died of the pox, her master had taken the woman's daughter, young as she was, into slavery in her place. When, daydreaming and tired of the hot work and the heavy iron, Joslyn had burned shirts, he had beaten her. When she complained of hunger, he had beaten her, and when she was so tired that her little eyes closed at the wringer, he had beaten her again. It had been a miserable life, but despite it, she was a happy little thing. And the sole keeper of my secret.

Of course, I kept my wings concealed from her. For many years, I wondered if she had forgotten. As a small child, she asked several times about them and why I had come to watch over her. When she was young, it was easier to let her think that I was an angel—her guardian angel—and I suppose that, for a time, I was.

Outside, it has grown dark, and lights begin to flicker in the village. It would be a nice village, were it not the place of my incarceration. It is a much smaller now than it was before they came. I cannot blame them for taunting me. It is the same with men who come to gaze in awe at the tiger once he is safely in a cage. To Vampires, I am a predator, a threat; I understand why they goad me. Nevertheless, the population of the village has dwindled because of them. They feed on the villagers to spite me, to remind me of my inability to perform the duties for which I am designed. I can no longer be called upon to send these fiends to a hell of their own making.

All but a few Vampires have chosen the life they lead, and even fewer choose to leave it voluntarily. For those who do, there is always Monsieur LeRay. A clever business, I must admit: a Cruxim charging to play mortician to Vampires who have grown weary of immortality. He set himself up in a dingy alley in Montmartre, open by appointment only. Most of his clients are simply tired: tired of life, tired of daily death, tired of the ever-changing world and their unchanging soul. Some are indeed remorseful, but all of them go knowing that no absolution awaits them. For those who do not wish to die, there is always me—should I ever escape this tower.

I return to my hideyhole and remove the blade again. I should get started, before they come. It is hard to hide my scraping from them once they arrive, flapping as they do around the tower. Often, they are disguised as bats, screeching, taunting me. I do not know how they found me here, but now they come often to mock me. Several times they have grown bold enough to attempt to fly in through the bars. But the bars are spaced too close to permit them entry, just as they deny me exit. If they could take the shape of any other creature, say the rat or the roach, they may be upon me while I slept, but they cannot. Even the wolf is beyond them. The bat is their only form of disguise. Many times I have wished that I too might take on the shape of an animal. If I could have, I might be with Sabine at this moment, instead of trapped in a tower.

THREE

Until the night I was captured, Sabine and I had spent every evening together since our first meeting on the streets of London some fifty years before. As she had finished eating, I stood watching until it began to rain: fat, black drops that washed the blood from the streets. Together, we had dragged the Vampire's corpse to the banks of the Thames near Blackfriars and set it adrift, and then we retired to the shadows of a nearby alley.

"What now?" I had asked. "Now that your charge is dead, you are a free agent."

"For now." She had effortlessly lain beside me on the doorstep and had absentmindedly begun to clean the blood from her body, licking at both white flesh and golden fur alike. "Although I would not call it free."

I watched, entranced. "Why not?" I asked, recognizing that this guardian was being most guarded and wondering what she had to hide; perhaps a great many things, given her lifespan.

She sighed and resumed her licking, wetting one great

paw with that delicate pink tongue and passing it fluidly over her chest and face. "I am being hunted."

"Hunted!" I laughed at the absurdity of it. "By whom?"

"My employer."

It had been a golden age for myth seekers back then. Everywhere, men had begun writing about shadows, seeking werewolves and harpies, Vampires and will-o'-the-wisps. It was all witches and pitchforks, God or the devil.

"I did not know any man knew Sphinxes were real." I gazed out at the rain and gave my wings a gentle flap to shake off the watery droplets.

"Nor did I," she admitted. "Until he found me."

"He?"

"Dr. Claus Gandler." She sighed. "Let us hope he never finds me again. His child, Fritz, had a rare illness. Polycythemia vera: an excess of blood. All his young life he bled—from the gums, from the nose, from the orifice, from the eyes. His father, Claus, was terrified they would come for him, and so he employed me."

"But how did he find you?"

"How do you think?" Her tail picked up the pace, as if she were frustrated by my stupidity. "He went to Egypt."

I smiled. "Of course."

I had never before seen a Sphinx, but nor had I ever expected to find one on the Continent. Perhaps that was naïve of me. Back in the day, I should have expected to find a Phix in Boetia. In Asia, it is possible I once walked straight past the inert, stone-cold gaze of a Nicolonia. But here? In London? Of course, everyone knew Egypt was the home of the Sphinx.

"How did he find you?"

"By mistake rather than by design. We are nocturnal. Being a creature of the night, you would know that." She turned her gaze from me and drew her tail forward, giving it a tender lick to clean the tip, the way a house cat might.

"You are statues by day?" I inquired, knowing it to be true.

"Correct. But our stillness is also our employ. Since time immemorial, we have been tasked with protecting the tombs of the newly dead from them, the undead. It began in Egypt in the far, far ages," she told me, using a phrase familiar to the very long-lived. "Vampires were few at first. The quality of the light, the dehydrating heat of the Old Kingdom did not suit them. But after an age, there was a plague of rats, followed by a plague of Vampires. When it was realized what they were and that they could take the form of bats, the Egyptians began to cleanse the streets of winged creatures, eradicate them even."

"I did not know that was a defense," I said, surprised.

"It is not." Sabine looked smug, then smiled. "But the Egyptians soon recognized that. Finding there was no way to curb such monsters' bloodletting, nor to kill them with any ease, they resorted to imprisoning them instead."

I remember the look in her eyes as she told me this: patience and wisdom, and a kind of gentle trust.

"The pyramids!"

Sabine just purred and stretched her back legs, getting comfortable. "Yes. At first. To begin with, the pyramids were nothing more than enormous, impenetrable prisons for Vampires. Later, they became tombs. But not for the Vampires. The Vampires interred within them withered but lived on. Perhaps some live on to this day, clinging to the walls in bat form, or as shrunken, skeletal monsters. No, the pyramids became tombs to protect the newly dead. The pharaohs and their families. The wealthy. The virtuous. The priesthood."

"To protect the dead from Vampires?" My eyebrows arched skeptically.

"Yes. But not from being eaten by them, from being turned by them."

"They can turn only the living," I said, a little too abruptly because Sabine growled in response before continuing.

"So say you, Cruxim." Her voice was gruff. "I thought you were sent to hunt them. To kill them." She fixed me with a steely gaze. "How can you not know they can turn a freshly cast-off body? For twenty-four hours after death, twenty-four hours alone, a Vampire is perfectly capable of turning the dead into the undead. A Vampire bite will animate the body within that first day of death, enough to allow the dead to feed on Vampire blood and rise up as one of them. Any longer than twenty-four hours, even a second more, and the corpse's cold blood congeals in the Vampire's veins, killing them instantly. Why do you think so many more Vampires immediately followed the Black Death?"

I had never been one to frequent cemeteries or morgues in search of the undead, although I suppose that might have seemed the obvious place to search for my quarry. On hearing that, all those years ago, I wondered why I knew so little about my enemy and myself. I knew that my ignorance compromised my mission.

I'd hesitated for a moment before answering. "That is the problem with being Cruxim, I suppose."

"You do not know these things?" she asked, disbelievingly.

I shrugged. "I work alone. My mother told me all Cruxim do. One of our many disadvantages. Whoever made us to combat them in many ways gave them the upper hand."

"You are as strong as they are," she said, and I noticed her eyes fly to my muscular arms.

"Yes. But they benefit from a culture. They are sociable creatures. For millennia, they have studied the lore that made them so. We Cruxim have no such library of knowledge about our mission, nor about our motive."

"How do you come to be then?" she asked, surprise pitching her voice higher than her standard purr. As she gazed at me expectantly, I realized she was attracted to me.

It caught me off guard.

I cleared my throat, embarrassed by her attraction and the feeling of my own blood hot in my veins. "We reproduce sexually." I looked down at the cobbles, ignoring her eyes. "But we never know our parents of the same sex. They die within hours of our birth."

She quirked an eyebrow. "Your population is unchanged then, constrained."

"Yes. I suppose it is." Even then, I had not known why I was telling her the secrets of my kind, or whether those whispers I remembered from my childhood were even true. Why open up to one I had just met, and one with the memory of a Sphinx, no less? "It is one of two ways a Cruxim is able to die—by giving life to another Cruxim."

"And the other way?"

I glanced at her sideways, wondering if she could be trusted. "To drink from a mortal, it is said."

Surprise flashed over her face. "So you were raised by your mother alone."

"At first. Within years she gave birth to my sister, and she too was lost to me when I was but a boy."

"Your sister's father would not take you in?"

"It is not our way, he told me. Once strong enough to hunt for ourselves, we do so alone."

Sabine had drawn air in through her fangs, and her tongue protruded slightly, comically, from between them. "You are at a disadvantage then, Cruxim. Your population remains constant, the older more experienced of your kind being constantly replaced with younger, more vulnerable Cruxim with little sense of history and no sense of lore. How have any of you survived?"

I nodded, disturbed by her assessment. "That is why Vampires turn humans. Not for company. The life of an immortal is lonely, but it is not for that. They do so to defeat us by number alone. To win."

Her gaze bored through me. "Where, then, did the Cruxim come from? Why are you here? Why are there not more of you?"

"I do not know. I am no conduit for my Maker. I do not even know him," I admitted. "I know only my purpose. I feel the need to hunt them, to feed off them. An insatiable thirst to kill." I shifted on the doorstep, feeling the warmth radiated by her fur. "How are you here?"

"I know neither." Her voice was proud, hard. "Nor do I care to. I am here. Perhaps I always have been. One day, I awoke from slumber and my limbs were no longer stone and my breath was no longer stilled."

"You just awoke from stone?"

She crossed her great paws one over the other. "That is all I know. Each day, when the sun rises above the horizon, I return to stone, not so much a location as an anchorpoint, tethering me to this world. My first guardian stone was limestone. Once, it rested outside the tomb of Pharaoh Ramesses IV, until it was moved to a museum, and now...." She trailed off, and her expression grew wistful. "Dr. Gandler must not find me when I am one with the stone."

It had stopped raining but had grown even darker, closer to the dawn. I stood to stretch my legs. "How did he find you the first time?"

"He realized what the pyramids truly were. The shape, like an inverted fang. The impenetrable nature of them. That they were places of imprisonment. He shares your passion for abolishing Vampires; such is his terror of them. Bringing Fritz to Egypt, he set out to search the African continent for any sign of them, to learn how he might exploit any weakness he discovered. The Sasabonsam and the Adze, the Impundulu and the Ramanga, Dr. Gandler found them all, studied them all—even managed to kill some of them. And then he found me."

She stopped to lick an affronting patch of fur on

her foreleg before continuing. "I had been entrusted to Ramesses tomb, as I told you, but he was long dead. The old days were gone. Where once the pyramids were living coffins in which to entrap Vampires, over time they became their refuges. The treasure hidden within kept them wealthy over centuries, and the labyrinthine passages and tombs became the perfect coven houses. My task became to deter them from coming, to guard the contents of the tombs. Dr. Gandler was granted special permission to visit the antechamber. But he did not leave with the rest of his research party."

"A brave man to stay in a pyramid by night."

"Or a foolish one." She yawned. The day was fast approaching. "But the fault is mine. I did not sense him somehow. If I had done nothing, they would have killed him. He would never have known me, never have been witness to my failure. Instead, I sprang out of the shadows to repel them, and in doing so, revealed myself to him. That was how he caught me the first time."

"Caught you?"

"Saw me. Threatened to expose me, to grind my anchorstone to dust, or to have it hurled into the sea. In return for his silence and my freedom, I had to honor his request that I guard his son."

"Fritz?"

"Yes. And so I did. I guarded the child for more than seven years, until he was in his early teens." She looked sad suddenly. "I even became quite fond of him. But in the end, it was no use."

"Vampires?" I avoided her gaze.

"Of course! Dr. Gandler was—is—furious. I abandoned my post momentarily to feed. A moment too long. Now, he is hunting me, and for a fate much worse."

I had scoffed a little at that, not to make light of her situation but in wondering whether she was being melodramatic. How, after all, did he intend to kill a Sphinx?

"Do not laugh, Cruxim—"

"Amedeo," I corrected her. "Call me Ame. And I laugh wondering how he intends to kill an immortal."

A low rumble issued from her throat. "Very well, Ame. Don't laugh. The esteemed Dr. Claus Gandler would no doubt love to entrap you too, as surely as he seeks to capture me. It is not death I fear: it is eternity in a cage."

Shutting off my memories again, I turn back to my task, freeing myself from the cage that has become my place of entrapment and of refuge from the monsters that have made the village their own. Only when I hear the swoosh of wings and the scratching of tiny claws scrabbling in the moss outside the window will I put the blade to rest. They have arrived. It will not be tomorrow, not now. Perhaps the day after.

"Oh, Angel," the voice comes from below, slippery with loathing. "Come to the window."

Beltran. I know his voice; how could I forget it? Many nights his words have come to roost in my head. His laughter, wild with condescension, a cuckoo in the nest of dreams I envisaged for Joslyn. I have promised myself that when I escape this tower, he will be my first scalp. I will toast my victory with his blood.

For the moment, of course, the victory is his, as it has been for more than two hundred years. I shake my head. Could it be true? Was it really that long ago? It still feels like yesterday.

FOUR

When Maria Del Santos died at the age of sixty-four, Joslyn was an orphan once more. The child was thirteen, as pretty a girl as you could hope to see, and as good and as clever as she was beautiful. I took her to the Convent de la Mare de Déu dels Àngels, outside the city, where I hoped she might spend her life in devotion to her Maker, as I did. At the very least, I thought she might be safe there, under the tutelage of Dominican nuns. And, for a time, she was.

As she grew older, my visits became more sporadic. I had a task to accomplish, which year upon year became harder. When I did visit, I was always stung by the sour looks of the nuns, as if they could sense a whiff of the preternatural on me. Many times, I considered their reaction had I allowed my wings to show: whether they would swoon in fervor or in fear of some bedevilment they could not comprehend.

The child, although at first considering me her guardian angel, no longer spoke of such things. I wondered if she even remembered the incident that had brought us together. Perhaps she had simply outgrown such childish fantasies.

Perhaps she believed Maria del Santos' lies and had come to think she was truly my illegitimate child, although she never called me Papa, preferring Ame.

Despite my absence, I wrote her often. She returned my letters, her childish scrawl soon giving way to the curling, sensuous writing of a young woman educated in philosophy, theology, Latin and French. And yet, her letters always made me melancholy. There seemed something unwritten in them, some sadness that was not shown to me when I visited.

No matter how busy I was, I made a point to visit at least once a year, on her birthday. Because the nuns frowned at expensive trinkets and the life of a would-be sister of the order demanded austerity, I bought her, every year, a book and a passionfruit. She had developed quite a taste for those delicacies from the New World, and their religious significance had the approval of the nuns. When I visited, we would stroll in the small arboretum attached to the convent or walk among the orange orchards and vegetable gardens while we talked. Sometimes, we would venture to a nearby brook or the ruins of an ancient castle in a glen a short walk from the convent.

"This is my favorite place, right here," she told me the year she turned sixteen. We were sitting in the castle, in the great hall, which had mostly escaped ruination but for the roof. "Here alone there is freedom." She fingered her rosary beads.

"Freedom?"

"Yes. You are lucky." Her eyes were downcast. "Your freedom is absolute. Infinite."

I had glanced up sharply at that, wondering if we were about to have a conversation I had anticipated for more than a decade. A conversation about why she aged but I did not appear to grow any older, about what I did for a living, about the wings she had once seen sprouting from my shoulders. But we did not. Not then, at least.

"We are all free in the love of our Lord and savior," I told her, unsure myself whether I believed it. Even then there were days when my servitude seemed a burden. Perhaps she felt the same. "Come now, we must go back." I put out my hand to pull her up.

Joslyn had looked at my hand for a moment and had then taken it, clasping it a little too tightly. When she rose, she did not let it go immediately. When we left the castle, she flung my hand away and hurried on ahead of me, her face flushed.

"Tell me," she asked abruptly, still facing forward.

I braced myself for the questions I anticipated, but all she said was, "Why did you bring me here?"

Ahead of me, her habit swished against a border of herbs, filling the air with fragrant rosemary. Even now, I associate the scent with her.

"For your safety," I said, honestly. "And so you could have an education."

She turned back to me and smiled sadly. "You could not have taken me yourself, given me the education you obviously have?"

I sighed, and I noticed her eyes flickered as she heard it.

"Why not?" she demanded, walking forward on the path again, her back to me. One of her hands was outstretched childishly, weaving through the flowering sage and rosemary, sending the bees dancing into the air. "You could afford it. You paid for this!" She flicked the other hand dismissively at her habit. "And I know you paid Mama to take me."

"That is untrue," I said sternly, thinking of Senyora del Santos and the support I had provided. "She always wanted a daughter."

Joslyn turned to me. "Well, she got what she wanted. But what about me? I always wanted a father. But you are not he. We both know you have never been my father."

"No." My voice trembled a little. "Joslyn, I have tried, in my way, to be like a father to you."

"No!" Joslyn gave a bitter laugh. Then, for some reason, she became angry. "Do not try! I have a father—our Holy Father. The only man I shall ever have. Not father. Not husband. Not son. You have made sure of that."

Perplexed by her outburst, I said nothing for several minutes, simply walked behind her in silence. Soon, I could tell by the set of her head and the stilling of the rosary that she had calmed.

I caught up and put my hand on her arm. "Forgive me. I have tried to do my duty as your guardian."

"Yes." Turning to me, she took my hand innocently in hers, the way she used to when she was a child. Her eyes softened with tears. "I must go back." She motioned toward the convent and then left me. As she turned to go, I thought I heard her whisper, "*El meu angel de la guarda.*"

The year after that she was more distant again, but I told myself it was just the way of girls growing into womanhood. Of course, we still wrote each other frequently, and when I visited we talked of art and theology, of life and of her sisters in the convent and their doings, but it was clear to me that something in our relationship was different. Occasionally, as we talked, I noticed she stole furtive glances at me. Perhaps I had changed after all. Or perhaps it was that I never changed. I did not ask. A woman's mind is her own place: a quarter men are excluded from. And a sister's mind, especially, belongs only to herself and God. *If something is bothering her, she will tell me*, I thought, not knowing then that, for women, the opposite is often true. Silences speak the loudest in a conversation between a man and a woman.

Sometimes, in her letters or during my infrequent visits to the convent, she would ask me about the world outside

Convent dels Angels. How did women dress in the streets, or how did they wear their hair? If her tone was a little wistful or her look a little faraway, I did not think it especially troublesome. I saw in those questions a vulnerability I did little to quash. It never occurred to me that a girl such as Joslyn, whose beauty bloomed more vividly each day and whose mind was as clear as my own, might not be happy in such a place. It never occurred to me in the slightest ... until that day.

It was the day of her nineteenth birthday. In the years since she had turned sixteen, I had become even more thankful for the habit she wore. There was something radiant about Joslyn, a glow that even the robes failed to diminish. At least, I told myself, the cloth kept her safe. Her purity was assured within the sanctity of the convent, if nowhere else. Nevertheless, I found myself struck by her beauty whenever I visited. When away from her, which I often was, I found myself impatient for her next missive. When a letter arrived it was read quickly, and then reread, and then kept with the others in a bundle by my bedside.

I was lonely, if you suppose; but it was more than that. Joslyn's tenderness softened the edges of a world that had grown cruel to me. The undead were everywhere. As fast as I killed one, as quickly as its blood quenched my hatred, another would take its place. They were organized by then, too, forming tight-knit covens and rarely venturing out alone. Although I had no shortage of prey, catching my quarry proved increasingly difficult.

The year she turned eighteen, Joslyn had written me that the convent had been attacked by brigands. One of the sisters, a girl named Sister Ermilita, had been killed in a field near the castle. Her body, when found, had been pale and anemic.

Some sort of animal, most likely a bat, Joslyn had written, *was thought to have been feasting on her blood. The sisters have cleansed the field of witchcraft, but visits to the ruined castle are forbidden. Where now will I find my time to be alone with just my thoughts? Where now will we find space to be alone together?*

I thought it an odd thing to write, since we were routinely alone together on my visits. Knowing how much she enjoyed our walks to the castle, I presumed she was just disappointed that one of her rare freedoms had been curtailed. I, too, was disappointed that the castle was off limits. I felt comfortable in ruins of any sort; for so many centuries, they had been a refuge. But when I reflect on it now, I must admit that it was more than that for me, too.

Joslyn had come to womanhood. Despite myself, I sometimes longed for a glimpse of her hair under the wimple or noticed the daintiness of her hands as she plucked a gardenia blossom from the garden and held it to her nose. The child she had been—the scabbed-kneed, scarred orphan—had been my charge, my duty. But the woman she had become was the source of my rare joy.

I have lain awake by day many times since, wondering what might have happened had things been different. Had she not done what she did. Had I reacted differently. But it is no use. What is done is done. And in our case, what was done will remain forever impossible to undo.

Still, despite the shame and regret that hangs over that day in my memory, I am unable to forget.

She was radiant that day. Her blue eyes, truer than the ever-changing Mediterranean, shone when I handed her the present I had bought her. It was an especially nice one that year: an illustrated, gold-embossed incunabulum of mythology I had taken from a coven-master I'd killed in Prague. I had fed deeply in Barcelona before coming to her, making my arrival later than usual. The sky had that gilt quality it gets just before sunset, which illuminated the book's cover as I handed her the gift. When she took it from me, her hand brushed mine. She looked up at me briefly and then quickly back down at the gift. Opening the heavy cover, Joslyn had stroked a slender finger across the hand-illustrated page, over the face of a Seraph that graced it. I remember how her long lashes cast crescents of shadow on the paper. She smiled up at me, but her eyes held a question.

I looked away quickly, afraid, myself, of the answer.

Although she never mentioned my place within the pantheon of angels and monsters, Joslyn had always been fascinated by mythology. Why I indulged her in it I do not know. In my own way, maybe I was bringing her closer to my true self, hoping—and yet simultaneously fearing—that one day she may really know me.

"And this," I said, holding out a bespeckled purple passionfruit, balancing its firm roundness on the palm of my hand like a suppliant presenting it before the altar.

Her hand wrapped around it on my palm, but she did not take it. She just stood there: palm clenched around the fruit, her dainty hand nestled on my open palm. Curling my own fingers around hers, I said, "Take it, it is yours," and squeezed her hand. But still she did not.

A moment passed between us.

She looked up at me, and her lips parted, as if to speak. I glimpsed an emotion in her I could not define. Then she snatched the fruit away with a mumbled, "Thank you," and hurried ahead of me on the path.

It was so unlike her, such ungracious behavior, that I questioned, "Joslyn?"

She did not answer but strode on down the path. Sometime later, she said without looking back, "Perhaps you will share it with me."

For years she had insisted I share the fruit with her; for years I had declined. Cruxim can eat, can even savor the richness of food, the velvet of claret or the biting fizz of champagne, and can even be sustained on them, but we do not require food or drink. Its enjoyment is marred by the superlative nourishment of blood. So, every year I declined, knowing her enjoyment of it would be a hundredfold my own. Still, every year she asked.

"No, you eat it. It is yours. I bought it for you."

She split the fruit's purple casing with a thumbnail. "You so rarely eat. You must take better care of yourself."

A frown creased my forehead. "I eat enough," I said, my thoughts flying to the body that lay in an alley near the Cathedral of Santa Eulàlia.

Joslyn put the fruit to her mouth and I heard her suck at it delicately as she continued making her way to the end of the arboretum, heading up the path that led to the castle.

I strode to catch up with her, seeing in this day some wildness that had lain dormant for the past six years. Approaching her, I reached out and put my hand on her shoulder. She shrugged it off.

"Joslyn?"

"What?"

As she turned to me, I noticed a sliver of passionfruit dribbled from the corner of her mouth—the black seed clinging in its yellow sac, which clung to her lips. Tenderly, I reached out to wipe it away. As I did so, she opened her mouth and caught my finger, gently sucking the sweet fruit from my fingertip.

At the touch of her lips, something leaped inside me. Her slow sucking thrilled me, and I pulled my finger out of her tongue's grasp too quickly, leaving a slurping gasp hanging in air between us as her lips drew air. Color flooded Joslyn's cheeks. Turning, she ran—awkwardly with her habit held up to expose her ankles—down the path toward the castle.

I, too, was embarrassed. I paused, replaying the moment in my mind, wondering what it all meant. Then, fearful for her safety, I pursued her. It was too late for her to be out alone. The mother superior would soon be calling her in for supper.

She was quick, even despite her robes and the encroaching darkness, and she was soon well ahead of me. My embarrassment burnished to anger. Had I not cared to be secretive, I would have flown ahead of her on the path. As it was, she made it to the castle before me.

The sun had slipped below the horizon by then, and the moon was not yet awake. In the half dark, the castle was a mess of awkward angles and long shadows that easily concealed a slim girl.

"Joslyn?" I wondered if she might have kept going, on to the brook.

There was no answer.

"Joslyn?"

Nothing answered but an echo.

Worried and growing weary of the game, my voice was stern when I called once more into the silence, "Joslyn!"

"Amedeo."

I had never heard her speak my full name before. Her letters were always addressed to "My Dear Benefactor," and in person, she always called me Ame. My name had a gravity on her lips that both excited and chilled me. I turned in the direction of her voice, pinpointing it to the shadows by one wall of the Great Hall. Even with my enhanced senses, it took a moment for my eyes to adjust to the darkness. "I am here." I stepped closer.

"Come closer," she murmured, moving into the thin light in the center of the room. She was paler than she should have been, and sylvan in the darkness. The silence that gripped me was the absent swish of her dark robes.

She was naked.

My breath choked in my throat.

Joslyn rushed towards me, her arms outstretched, her

face framed by hair mussed by the removal of her wimple. How I had longed to see her hair, and yet now it terrified me. It gleamed dark as sin in the rising moonlight, unaware of its power.

Ignorant of my reaction, Joslyn rushed on until her body met mine. I felt her arms around my neck, her breath warm on my cheek.

"Amedeo," she whispered.

A ripple of sensation rose in me at hearing my name again on her tongue.

It did not last.

Joslyn's mouth quickly moved to my mine. She pressed her lips to my mouth, and I tasted passionfruit over the headiness of desire. My hands rose to her hair, silkier than my wings' down. Unconsciously, I knotted a skein of it around my hand, pulling her closer still, my lips parting in turn.

Then guilt overtook me. "Joslyn," I said, weakly at first. Then, coming to my senses, "Joslyn!" Taking her by the shoulders, I pushed her back, holding her at arms' length.

She blinked, her lips still parted, her mouth ripe with desire.

I suppose part of me immediately regretted stopping her. My eyes, used to the dimness of the Great Hall, now lingered on her coltish thighs, the cello fullness of her hips, and then that face—that lovely face with blue eyes brimming now with tears.

Seeing the movement of my eyes, Joslyn brought her hands up to cup the crest of her breasts, which served only to make them more prominent.

Finally, disgusted with myself, I looked away, stammering, "Y-your habit. Where is it?"

"Why?" She laughed, a quiet, defeated laugh. "Amedeo, why?"

"Because you're naked, that's why!"

She laughed again, bitterly this time. "Yes. I am naked. I am a woman. Does it surprise you so, my beloved Benefactor? Do you think me still a child cooing over dolls?"

"No. I..." My eyes fell again to her body and then away. "I think you a novice. A sister of the cloth!" I dropped my hands from her shoulders and took a step back.

"If only that were it." Her sigh escaped like a bat into the night. "I am a novice only because you put me here. Like a marionette I cannot dance unless you bade it. Why did you cloister me, Ame? You do not want me but do not want anyone else to have me. Is that it? You would deny me the love of any other? Of someone who may love me back?" Her voice was thick with tears.

"Joslyn!" Her name came out more harshly than I intended. "Do not speak such things. I have always loved you. You know that."

"Like a father?" she asked. "We both know that is not your kind of love."

"I protect you!"

"Ah, yes." She looked away. "My guardian angel."

I simply stared at her, not knowing what to say.

She returned my stare and then pushed closer again. Grabbing my shirt, she tore it roughly at the shoulder. Her hand slid down my back, seeking the softness she knew she would find there. "Did you think I had forgotten this?" Plucking out a feather, she said, "You think you can fool me that you are my father. You are not even a man!" She held the feather before her, a droplet of blood at its base. "You bleed like a man." Her blue eyes frankly assessed my body, noting my arousal at her nearness. "Desire like a man, even. But you ... what are you, Amedeo? An angel who is incapable of love?"

Still I was mute.

"Oh, Ame." She stroked my cheek with the feather.

I turned to the side, struggling to resist her.

"For years I have loved you—only you. Why else did I write you, long for your visits and for your words? I dreamed one day you would come and take me from this place, to somewhere we could be together."

"Joslyn," I said again, less firmly.

Her eyes were glassy with tears. "How foolish of me, to want so badly a love that cannot hope to last even one of your lifetimes. And so I thought that perhaps, just for an instant, you might indulge me." She ran the feather from my cheek to my collarbone, her other hand flying to the buttons on the front of my torn shirt. "That, just for once, I might know what it is to be a woman before I must learn what it is to be a nun."

"Joslyn, this is foolishness." I clasped her by the wrists, holding them firm against my chest. I could feel her pulse in them, the blood-beat as intoxicating as her nearness.

"Just a kiss then." She was sobbing now. "One kiss to remember you by." Involuntarily, my grip softened. Her hands flew to my chest and one crept around my back to stroke my right wing. She raised her face to me again, and I bent my head to her, knowing that her closeness was too much, her power over me too great. I could not do this. Should not do this!

I leaped backward, tearing angrily at my shirt and exposing my wings. "Joslyn, go home!" I commanded in a tortured voice. "This is not for you!"

"What is for me? A life of misery and seclusion with tired old women, that is what you want for me?"

In the corner, I spotted her abandoned habit. With a great flap of my wings, I flew to it, clutched it up, and threw it on the floor at her feet. "A life of purity!" I said. "Not this ... this seduction like a common harlot. Go home!"

I could bear it no more. The temptation of her was too great. With another almighty flap, I soared up in the air before her. Although tormented by the thought of leaving her naked and alone, I knew I was not strong enough to stay.

"GO BACK!" I commanded, swooping out through the ruined roof and into the cool dark arms of the night.

Below me, Joslyn crumpled to the floor. Her body gleamed pale against the black cloth of her habit. "It is as it ever was," she cried. "When I need you, you fly away. I hate you."

I knew then, and only then, that her love for me was true.

Angry at myself and at her, I soared over the fields, flying rapidly with little thought of who or what might be abroad to see me so early in the evening. Only when I reached a lonely elbow of the brook did I stop. Landing, I then threw off my clothes and waded in up to my waist. A naked angel bathing in the moonlight. Even the cold water did little to still the waves of desire and anguish that flooded through me. How had I missed it? Her unhappiness. The change in her. And was she right? Had I been so callous as to deny Joslyn her liberty for my own purpose? Had I wanted no one else to have her?

Yes, I quickly realized: that much was true. But nor could I reconcile our relationship. This child-woman who for the past fifteen years had needed my protection needed it still. My heart knew I must save her from myself as much as from others.

I ducked under the water. Small fish darted before me as I splashed my wings in frustration, sending droplets of quicksilver into the air. My hands to my wet hair, I wept, knowing then what I must do. I must set her free and leave her. She was a woman now, and my protection had become her prison. Gradually, an uneasy calm returned to me, and then, more than an hour later, I returned to the castle.

I arrived to find the ruins illuminated by some light I could not recognize and swooped down, landing outside the walls. *Joslyn must have somehow concealed a lantern,*

I thought. As I approached, the fickleness of the light wavered on the gilt cover of the incunabulum I had given her and alerted me that she had lit a fire.

"Joslyn?" I flapped down through the ceiling into the room adjoining the Great Hall. There was little smoke, but a noise caught my attention, a muted scrabbling. Perhaps a rat or a bat, I thought as I hurried closer to the flickering glow, keeping to the shadows a little, lest she still be upset with me.

I saw her foot first, stretched out taut on the cold cobbles of the castle floor. Her robes and wimple were beneath her. I remember still the pointed elegance of her toes, the curve where her other leg, drawn up in the air, became buttock.

The rest of her nakedness was hidden to me. The broad back of the man above her obscured her nudity. Dark hair swung on his shoulders as he gyrated above her. Muscles tensed, he leaned down to kiss her neck, his hands upon her wrists.

I watched for just seconds—rage and jealousy blinding me—before I rushed forward. "Joslyn!"

Her whimper of desire was drowned by a scream of laughter as the Vampire turned toward me. Blood dripped from his fangs and speckles of it shot forward in the firelight as he hissed. Then he jumped away from her.

Joslyn's eyes sprang open, and her hand reached out for him. "Beltran," she said breathlessly, and I noticed that her teeth too were stained with blood.

It was then that I knew it. Aside from the flushed cheeks, the low-lidded eyes, the hair a nest from writhing, against the paleness of her neck was a dark smear of blood.

"NO!" I spun around, propelling myself towards the Vampire with all the speed my still-drying wings could manage. "You have NOT done this!"

"Au contraire, Cruxim." Beltran leaped up, clinging to the walls of the castle with his long nails. "She begged me to."

His laugh brought bile to my throat.

"How could I resist a virgin, let alone a nun?"

Joslyn sprang to her feet. "Ame!" she commanded, and then, with just a hint of shame, said, "Leave him. What he says is true. I ... I ... I wanted to know what it was like."

Striding to her, I seized her head in my hand, turning it roughly to the side. The smear became a trickle, a rivulet of blood from two puncture wounds in her throat. "And this?" I asked hoarsely. "You would be a whore and a monster?"

Joslyn wrenched her head from my hands, and her stare was haughty. I knew, in that moment, that she was no longer human.

"I would be an immortal. Like you," she said.

"No," I managed through gritted teeth. I pointed to where Beltran, naked and still sniggering, clung to the castle wall. "Like him!"

Her voice became gentle then, and her eyes softened. "Please," she said, clutching at my arm. "I did it for us, that we may always be together. That you might love me now for eternity."

"You have no idea what you have done!" I flung her away, my desire to kill her stronger than any other, except perhaps my desire to weep for her. "I brought you here, to God"—I swung an arm in the direction of the convent— "and you have plunged yourself straight to hell. Don't you understand what I am? What you are now? We can never be together. Never."

Her face crumpled. She pointed to Beltran. "But he said..."

"He said. He said!" I raged. "He is the devil's apprentice, the evil I have sought to protect you from. And failed." Spinning on my heel, I launched myself up the wall, my arms seeking the jugular of my enemy. Beltran, his feet bunched against the wall, leaped away to cling on the opposite side, and bared his fangs.

"If you catch me, you can have me, Cruxim," he goaded.

"Just like I had her."

I flew at him again, in my rage slamming hard into the bare wall he had vacated, winding myself slightly.

"Ame!" Below us, Joslyn crumpled on her robes and hugged her knees to her chest. Tears of blood sprang from her eyes.

"You will kill me," Beltran said, "and leave her a newborn. No longer a virgin nun but assuredly a virgin Vampire alone in a world of infinite pain with no one to instruct her in how to survive. Oh, Cruxim, you are harder than I thought. Or will you kill her now? I know you can feel her. I know you want her. I can assure you she tastes good." Beltran licked his lips theatrically.

"Stop it!" Joslyn sprang to her feet again. "Stop it both of you."

My laugh was a thing of despair as it echoed around the chamber. "Stop what? This?" I gestured wildly to Beltran, to myself. "This can never be stopped. This is my purpose: to kill Vampires in the name of God. His"—I pointed to Beltran—"is to make them in the name of the devil. You wanted a lover, well you have one now. Lust as hot as hellfire for eternity. Are you happy?"

"No," she whispered, and I saw that it was true: already she was miserable. She would have eternity to get used to it. Abandoning my hunt for Beltran, I fluttered down beside her.

"Ame." Joslyn rushed to embrace me.

That one last time, fighting my deepest urges, I had let her. I had drawn her into my arms, feeling her head on my shoulder, smelling the fragrant, musty warmth of her, the rosemary and passionfruit and sex that clung to her hair and hands. I had considered plunging my fangs into her neck then and there, saving her from a lifetime of horror. Yet nor could I condemn her to the hereafter.

"Go with him," I said gruffly, releasing myself from her embrace. I pushed her back, in the direction of Beltran. "Go from this place. From me. I must never see you again." Using every ounce of my strength, I laid a kiss upon her brow. She was as cold as stone, yet that kiss burned like a brand on my lips. "I must never see you again," I repeated. "If I do, I will kill you both."

I flew directly upward, not looking back, ignoring Beltran's laughter and Joslyn's wracking sobs. I flew for many, many miles that night, stopping only when my eyes were devoid of tears.

I told Sabine little about her. I do not know why. I suppose she might not understand, might be jealous even. Maybe not of my love for Joslyn, tightroping between the love of a child and of a woman, but of Joslyn herself: the legs and arms and body parts that compose a mortal woman. Or she might think me weak, that I did not kill them both that night. Many times since, I have had the same thought. Instead, I left my charge in the care of a killer, and one of the worst kind. Ah, regrets, I have so many. The one thing longevity bestows.

Sabine, in her infinite wisdom, never asked. Not about any others. For more than a century, that was enough. I was able to make her believe there was no one else in my heart. Mostly, there was not—nothing but a dull ache where Joslyn's love used to nestle. But my heart was never the problem, nor hers. Nor was it any other lover that came between us.

I had slept with a mortal only once, when I was but a boy. I kept my coat on and lay on the bed, letting her writhe above me. I know the effect I have on mortal women, and she was satisfied. As for Vampires, never. My dealings with them are only in death.

Ironically, it was the very thing I loved about Sabine that prevented me from loving her entirely.

"You love me like an artifact," she had growled at me.

"I may as well be eternal stone." Her tail flicked erratically, and she prowled back and forth, growling. "Then we can be stone together."

They were the last words she had said to me before she vanished inside the stone that acted as her anchor, daily drawing her from the physical realm. She would not tell me where her anchorstone—as I learned the guardians called it—was located, so fearful was she of Dr. Gandler. I had a hint that it was in a small collection somewhere, in a dusty, private museum where it received little attention, but I could not be sure. I still cannot. She told me once that if I kissed the stone, her eyes might open, but I was unsure whether she was telling the truth. Even if I were out of this tower, I might not be able to find her unless she wanted to be found.

She was right: I was unfeeling. Was it out of some remnant loyalty to Joslyn that I could not give Sabine what she desired? I do not think so. I loved Sabine. I love her still.

"You love the idea of me," she had angrily suggested one earlier time, when we had the same argument.

I had stopped, considering her words. "No." I responded. "I love you, Sabine."

"Then prove it." She had lifted her head to meet my gaze, and her eyes burned to a lustrous topaz as she padded towards me. It was early evening. We had both just fed together on a Vampire I'd caught loitering outside a bar. I had removed my blood-soaked shirt and Sabine had spent the better part of an hour cleaning her fur, stopping occasionally to nuzzle and kiss me playfully or to bat me away with her great paws.

"Show me," she said, and her voice was velvet, contrasting with the roughness of her tongue on my bare stomach.

She had pounced, knocking me playfully to my feet. Her eyes flashed as she stood over me, and then she bent her head to my neck. The gentleness of her kiss belied her strength. I placed my arms around her, propping myself on my wings, feeling the softness of her wings above me, larger and more heavily feathered than my own. With a sigh of happiness, she flapped them playfully, and I lifted my body up again to kiss her, my hands falling to her breasts.

I must pause for a moment in my retelling to remember them, for they were perfect. There was no wonder in my mind that the creator has chosen to make them forever bare. Each was perfectly turned, its roundness culminating in a pyramid of rosy nipple.

I had brought my lips to each, feeling Sabine's resonant purr through them. All around me, her mane of blonde hair, the sleekness of her fur. She dropped on top of me, kissing my face, allowing my hands to move along her back, to stroke her flanks. The cushioned softness of her paws pinned me down. Sabine had groaned again and bitten me, an involuntary nip of pleasure as I continued my adoration of her body. Then her haunches bunched, her back claws extended to grip the rooftop below us, and she growled again. The full moon cast snakelike shadows of her erect tail as it lashed from side to side. Had I not known better, I might have thought she were angry with me. The low growl came again, fragmented by her purr, and she kissed me even more deeply—so deeply I felt the points of her canines glance my lip.

"Ame," she rumbled and wriggled herself forward again, the weight of her, and the sensual turn of her lips nearly robbing me of breath.

With all the strength I could muster, I pushed her away.

She playfully resisted, catching my face in her paws and kissing it again before recognizing my hesitance. With a quick movement, she hauled herself up and off me and crouched as if to spring. "What is wrong?"

I avoided her gaze, focusing instead on the twitching of her tail.

Noticing the movement of my eyes, she sat down and curled her tail forward around her haunches. The lust in her eyes turned to shame, and her purr died in her throat. "So that is it," she said, her eyes downcast. "That is how you see me?"

"You cannot know how I see you," I answered.

A frown crossed her brow, and her beautiful full lips drew into a tight, pink line. "I know that you see a beast in place of a beauty. I know that you will never let me love you as I desire."

I sighed. "Sabine..." I took a step closer. She was always difficult to approach when wounded, and I was tentative. "You are beautiful to me."

"Am I?" she spat. "Oh, parts of me are beautiful to you. But this," she lashed her tail. "This!" She stretched, that way cats do with both of their hind legs extended rigidly behind them. "This is animal. This is beast. Beast! That is how you see me. Like all of the rest. A freakshow. Or nothing but a pet."

"Sabine." I tried to reassure her.

"You do not know," she spat. "You cannot know what it is like to forever be half beast." She sprang away into the night, denying me the chance to tell her that I did; that perhaps all men know that.

It was not the first time the argument had arisen, but the night before my imprisonment, it would be the last.

I have thought, many times, about why I could not take that final step with Sabine. It was not out of revulsion but a sense of moral wrongness: the same gut feeling that cast a wall between Joslyn and me. Once she left, that final night of our togetherness, I wondered what was wrong with me. Was it my destiny to deny myself the things I most wanted? Or was it not me denying them, but something greater than myself?

FIVE

"You should see her now," came his voice again from below the tower. "More beautiful than even you could ever have guessed. But I heard that you go for beasts now." His laugh was strident. "Shall I send a little beastie up there for you?"

The squeal of bats was followed by another laugh. "Be a good Cruxim, and let the little bat in. It won't eat much."

"Do you forget, Beltran, my last words to you?"

"I am a Vampire, Monsieur. We never forget."

"Then you will not forget this: one day, I will be released from this tower, and when I am, I will put your head on a pike, along with every other hell-bound member of your coven. I will burn you all, a baptism for your final resting place."

"Every member, Cruxim?" He laughed uproariously. "I will tell her that when I get home. Oh, Cruxim, it will break her heart."

"Do not speak to me of hearts," I thundered. My voice bounced off the walls of the chamber and flew out to greet him. "Let not the heartless talk of hearts."

"Or the loveless of love." A peal of laughter followed his words up the walls. "I like you like this, Cruxim. Such a pussycat. A caged lion. Just like your lover."

Had he found Sabine? Surely not or Beltran would have paraded her before me. It was a taunt, nothing more.

"Be careful, Devil," I yelled. "It is the lioness who hunts. She may kill you before I do."

A snort floated up from below. With a screech, a rain of bats descended on the window, battering their wings against the bars, their cries piercing the night.

It was not the next day, nor the next. The chip of stone lay sullen and untouched in its hideyhole. The girl did not come again.

She was replaced by an ancient, stooped man in a black hood. He sat at the top of the stairwell for the entire first day of his watch, his wrinkled face shadowed by the hood, impassive. My attempts to engage him in conversation were met with silence. I could do nothing while he was there but watch. All the while, I longed for the solitude to continue my plan.

The second day, he took an object from a leather satchel he carried. The flip of the pages drew my attention. It had been four decades since I had read a book, and the thought came sorely to me. I remembered the embossed incunabulum I had given Joslyn and wondered what had become of it. Walking to the bars, I asked, "You are a reader?"

Finally, the man spoke. "A reader. A researcher. A collector, if you like."

"What do you collect?"

He raised his head, revealing his eyes for the first time. They were a deep onyx, endless as an abyss, and the only spark of life in his gray face.

"Curiosities." He closed the book with a snap, and I saw a gleam of gold on the ancient cover.

A chill rippled through me.

"Aren't you curious?" he asked.

I shrugged. "Isn't everyone?"

"Indeed." Opening the book again, he turned to a page and held it up to me. "Tell me, what do you make of this?"

I looked at the page and then immediately whirled away in surprise. Then, checking myself, turned back to face him. "An age-old myth," I said. "The Sphinx."

"A myth? Just a story in an old book?" He traced the gilt image with his finger and blew away dust. "I wonder," he lingered over the words, "given they're so prominent in mythological literature, from Greece to Egypt to Asia, whether there might not be some truth in them. But then, I'm just a man." He studied me, his expression not of curiosity but of knowing.

I said nothing.

"Tell me"—he approached the bars—"as a Seraph, do you think they exist."

I was taken aback. Who was this man? Or rather, what? I maintained my silence.

The man flipped forward several pages and held the book up again. Depicted was a Cherub. One gray, overgrown eyebrow shot up toward the old man's balding pate.

I remained silent.

"I know what you are," he whispered through the bars.

"Apparently not." I turned my back on him to face the window, thankful my coat hid my wings.

"Perhaps you are a type of Vampire? Nosferatu?" He changed tack.

"Keep guessing, old man." He was beginning to annoy me.

"I suppose I could always ask Sabine."

Despite myself, I spun around and tore over to the bars.

"So." He chuckled. "You have made her acquaintance after all."

"How do you know her?"

"I told you: I collect curiosities."

"And Sabine?"

"I'm sure you will agree she is a curious beast."

"Gandler!" The name came to me in a flash of memory. "What have you done with her?"

"Done? Nothing. I can take you to her if you like, if you will let me bind you. If you will come willingly."

I considered it for a moment. At the very least, it would mean a temporary freedom from this prison, but from Sabine's tale, Dr. Claus Gandler could not be trusted. Perhaps he did not even have Sabine, although how he had discovered I knew her, I did not know. Was it a lucky bluff?

I stared at him again. His black eyes were fixed on me. One finger casually smoothed the page of the book.

"If Sabine knows I am here, why didn't she come herself?"

Gandler laughed. "In the daytime? I'm sure you know as well as I that by day she is ensconced in stone."

"Yes," I said. "In Alexandria." I made a wild guess, hoping beyond hope I was wrong. I was sure Sabine would never return to Egypt, not while Gandler remained alive.

Dr. Gandler's eyes lit up, and his nostrils flared. It was enough to tell me he did not have Sabine. He was fishing.

"Alexandria," he repeated thoughtfully.

I laughed, all the while calculating in my head. Fifty years had I known Sabine. Gandler must be in his late eighties at least. I hoped his mortal life would be snuffed out before he laid eyes on Sabine again. If it had not been for the bars, I might have considered snuffing it out myself, even though to do so would mean death for me.

"You will not come with me, then?"

"Old man, if you open that door, it will take more than bindings to keep me from your throat."

The laugh that came from him rasped with age. "You supernaturals, always so melodramatic. Suit yourself. Enjoy your prison." He creaked to his feet, clapped the book shut, and shook it at me. "I found this," he told me, "in the ruins of a castle near Barcelona when I was but a boy. It is very old they tell me. Hundreds of years. Such a shame what the weather did to it, but I have had it restored as best I could. It would have been very beautiful once. But it has been a most helpful guide to your preternatural kin. I wonder if the original owner found it as useful. It was inscribed to a woman named Joslyn. With a bit of digging through the convent archives, I was able to discover it belonged to a novice, it turns out. An orphan—poor thing. The convent records said she vanished one night, something to do with a strange benefactor. Curious, isn't it?"

"Among a lifetime of curiosities, perhaps not so much." I yawned. "Now, if you don't mind."

He squinted through the bars. "I don't know what you are." His voice was menacingly quiet. "Not yet. But I know who you are. I have seen one like you once, just a fleeting glimpse of her face in the crowd, but it was enough to make me want her. And I will find Sabine too, and you ... well ... you're not going anywhere just yet, are you?" He turned and made his way down the stairs.

"I'm not going anywhere, Gandler," I yelled after him. "But you are. You're going to hell, you whoreson. Say hello to Fritz."

For an old man, he was back up the steps faster than I anticipated. He grasped the bars in his withered hands and shook them fiercely. Pinpoints of light in his black pupils shone like daggers as he spat, "You'll regret that. You and that on-heat she-bitch you call a lover." He rattled the bars again.

It was only then that I realized he never had the key.

As soon as he left, I retrieved the flint, more determined than ever not to be there when he returned. *With some luck, he's already on his way to Alexandria*, I thought, although something told me he was smarter than that.

I couldn't tell what bothered me more: that he knew about Sabine or that he had Joslyn's book. I had inscribed the gift in the front, simple words that told her nothing of my love for her. I wondered that she hadn't taken it with her. Then my mind flew back to that night and the state she had been in. I remembered Beltran, clinging naked to the wall, mocking me, and her deflowered and trembling, weeping. And then it did not seem so unlikely that she had forgotten. Perhaps her interest in the book's content had waned. What good is it to read about ghouls and wraiths once you have become one?

My black thoughts suited the task at hand, and I chipped away until the sun began to inch its way through the cracks in the mortar and set the sparrows stirring. A thin wedge of stone prevented me from breaking through entirely. Tomorrow would be the day. Soon, the hole I had created would be big enough for me to put both feet in, and then I would kick my way to freedom. Content in that knowledge, I curled up in the corner of my cell and slept. I dreamed of Sabine.

When I awoke, the squeal of bats heralded the night.

Six

The stone squeaked beneath my exertion but did not budge. I put all of my strength into it, all of my will, and I felt the grinding and shifting beneath my feet and smelled the mustiness of the moss shearing away on the wall outside. Close to sunset as it was, bright sunlight still pierced my chamber—the first in decades—and my senses sang.

I was free.

I did not stop to consider the strength of my wings or body, simply slithered on my belly to the hole I had created and ran my hands lovingly over the gap where the stonework had plummeted. It was man-sized; I was sure of it.

Don't be a fool, Ame, my thoughts whispered. You should wait for daylight. Go out when your prey is asleep and at its most vulnerable. It had been so long since I had hunted that I knew my own advice was sound, yet I thought of Sabine, confined to her anchorstone by day, and propelled myself out anyway. My hands grasped for the vines that covered the tower, hoping they might support my weight. As soon as I was outside, I understood my folly. The walls were slippery, the vine weak, and the masonry so eroded it could barely withstand even my scarce weight. I had thrown off my coat in the process of working, leaving my wings free, but they were unpracticed. Decades of strength had seeped out of me. An experimental flap revealed that my wings were barely functional.

As the sunlight began to fade, I clung to the tower wall several hundred furlongs up, wishing I had taken my own counsel. When the vines gave out, I plummeted like the stones I had kicked out earlier, my wings doing little but break my fall.

Freedom is a peculiar thing. For decades, I had craved it, but now that I had it, it meant little to me without Sabine. And where to find her, I knew not. I guessed she would not have returned to Egypt, but whether she was in London, Prague, Greece, or elsewhere, I did not know. Had she remained here in France? Perhaps she had made her way to the New World, where old creatures might find some respite from their past.

When my wings had recovered some of their former strength, I flew to Paris and prowled the streets in search of her. Examining rooftops. Staring at gargoyles. Looking always for a Sphinx-shaped sculpture that might reveal her to me. But nothing did.

In one such street, in the enveloping darkness, something slim and black fled from me in terror. I recognized the scent and the sylvan movement—one of them. Exhausted and weak as I was, I followed. The creature's blood smelled rich, warm, and compelling, and my old urges overtook me. He turned, his face a mask of terror as he fled before me. Suddenly, I saw that, strangely, he was little more than a child. It was rare for covens to entertain the thought of one so young. The knowledge threw me, but not enough. Part of me felt a surge of pleasure in it: he would be an easy meal. But it was not to be. He sprinted down an alley that appeared a dead end. I followed, expecting to corner him there, but instead he knocked sharply on a heavy oaken door set into the wall. It was flung open and just as quickly slammed upon his entry.

A coven house. Beltran! I thought, wondering if this were indeed the address of my nightly tormentor. If so, he would discover tonight that I had flown. Soon, the entire coven would be on guard for me. If I attacked tonight, it would afford me surprise, but I was in no state to take on a nest of Vampires.

Defeated, I slunk away and fluttered to a rooftop. After I had dined on a nest of owls, I made a bed for the night in the Cathedral of Notre Dame. There would be time enough for vengeance.

Vengeance found me on the morrow, long before I sought it out. Shortly after dusk, I noticed a blur of motion in the shadows. I was groggy, still half asleep, and I realized by then how vulnerable I was. Saying nothing, I crept forward. The mewling of a kitten stalled me for a moment, but what I had seen was bigger than that, and stealthier. A dull moan issued from a shadow to my right.

"Who goes there?" I pressed myself against the sandstone wall at my back.

"Someone you well know."

I knew the voice. With a hiss, I rushed from the shadow, my fangs exposed, wrists grasping for his neck.

"Cruxim, Cruxim, Cruxim." Beltran tsked. "Did you think to escape and then menace my boy with no retribution?" His pale, handsome face emerged from the shadows like a wraith. "Really," he said, "it is little wonder your kind is all but extinct."

I leaped forward with a snarl, but he stepped aside and to the left. "Temper. Temper. Calm yourself. I bring you a gift."

"Your blood be my gift." I hurled myself toward him again.

He sighed, and the sudden whites of his eyes gleamed in the darkness. "Not that. This..." In the half-light he thrust forward a woman, her head down. Long dark hair covered her face. "You said you wanted to kill her, said you wanted to kill all of us. So do it. It is what she wants. Isn't that so, Joslyn?"

The woman gave a thin, high-pitched sob, and nodded.

"Tell him, then." Beltran shook her.

I took in her height, her hair, the bearing of her body. She looked up at me, and even in the semi-darkness I could tell her eyes were azure. My heart quickened.

"Ame," she said, and her voice sounded strained.

Any sense of the stirring I had felt when she said my name all those centuries ago had withered in me. I wondered at that; I had thought about her every day. *You promised her death*, I reminded myself, *if you ever saw her again.* An angry beast deep within me seemed to growl at the memory.

"I cannot live like this," she whispered. "The killing..."

A twinge of pity piqued me. Then I remembered what she was asking me to do. "And yet you come to me and ask me to kill."

"It would be a mercy."

I flew to her, astonished by the strength of my anger after all these decades. Grasping her arms, I gazed into her face. Dark shadows hung beneath her eyes, and I noted with sorrow that much of her beauty had fled. She looked a different girl, so changed was she. *She is a corpse already,* I told myself, and a renewed rage coursed through me. "Monsieur LeRay is a mercy." I shoved her away. "I assure you, I would be no such thing."

She groaned then, a pitiful noise. "But this life, Ame. This life is hell."

My laugh, equally pitiful, echoed down the cobbled street, but inside my heart ached for her. "Hell!" I said. "Where do you think you will go, if I do this?"

She cried then and hung her head.

"Come, Cruxim, you promised. I told her I would bring her to you. That I had found you. She has searched for so long. Always searching for you, despite everything." Beltran shoved her forward, and she toppled over, crying into the cobblestone. "Despite how that made me feel," Beltran continued. "Come, you always wanted her. She is yours."

"I am yours," she pleaded. "Please, please kill me. This … this is torture."

Some better part of me could not bear to see her like this, but the baser animal in me saw it as either a justice or a mercy. Or maybe even a duty. She was part of my mission now; she had chosen her path.

I knelt beside her and stroked the dark hair from her neck. She was warmer than I thought she would be, or was I remembering it? The dead were usually cold, so bitterly cold, but it had been so long since I had fed, I might have imagined it. It had been so long since I had touched another person.

Joslyn groaned and rolled toward me, clutching at my legs, curling her body around them. I had a fleeting memory of her as a child. "This will be forever," I choked out.

"Better that forever than this one," she sobbed.

I slid down onto the cobbles beside her, my arm over her, and pressed my lips to her neck. It was warm, wet with a sheen of perspiration. A finger of foreboding crept up my spine.

"Wait!" A thunderbolt of fawn shot from the shadows. With a yowl, it threw itself at Beltran, a tangle of claws and tumbling curls.

"Sabine!"

Beltran, caught unawares, was thrown off his feet. With a scream, the girl leaped to her feet, too. Seeing Beltran knocked to the ground, she turned and fled.

"Joslyn, wait." I caught at her sleeve, tearing it. Only then did I notice what should have been obvious. Her wrist and arm were marred with bite marks, black and swollen like the pox.

"You are human!" As I said it, the veil of sorcery slipped away and I realized this was not Joslyn at all. Turned women were beautiful, gleaming, ethereal. She was human, nothing but a plaything of the darkness. The terrified look on her face confirmed my thoughts.

She is right. Better death than an existence of being fed upon daily by monsters.

She turned and fled into the jumble of streets.

Behind me, I heard Sabine's guttural growl as she flew at Beltran, but he was quicker than she and leaped out of her claws' reach.

"Sabine!" I cried again.

She paid me no mind, her eyes fixed on him and burning with contempt. I hardly had time to admire her—the supple, muscular agility that enabled her to leap onto a wall after her quarry—before I was assailed from behind and the bloodlust rose up in me, crested and urgent. I spun to find more of them advancing on me, their teeth drawn.

"What was she?" I growled. "Your harlot? A living meal? Do any of you even know where Joslyn is? Who she is?"

"Oh, I believe Beltran knows," a thin, blond Vampire sneered. "I believe he knew her well … in the biblical sense." He let out a braying laugh that ended abruptly as my hand crushed his pale throat. His death came with a gurgling laugh and the launch of another Vampire at my shoulders. I whirled and shrugged, shaking that one off too and throwing him to the ground before bringing my heel down hard on his jaw. Then I fell upon him and quickly drank, feeling the life rush back into me, the hatred, the anger, the purpose, all of the feelings that had been boxed up with me in my cell.

I will kill you all. But could I really? If she were here, could I take her from them? Could I lose her all over again? I did not want to find out.

In the background, I heard Sabine snarl, and I spun to find her advancing on Beltran once more. He was up against a wall, the thick wet moss at his back. Sabine's top lip curled, and her eyes gleamed hatred as she stalked toward him.

"Shhhh, pussycat," he mocked her. "Come now, my pet, and lie down before me. My, my, won't you make a lovely skin on a cold floor. Or perhaps a cloak."

I heard her hiss again as I drew closer. "Sabine," I called. "This is not your quarrel. He is mine. I promised him that."

Beltran turned his attention to her, but I could tell by the stiffness of his pose that it was me he expected, not Sabine.

She leaped towards him, but he was agile as a knife. His teeth gleamed in the moonlight as he taunted her from the top of the wall.

"Here kitty, kitty, kitty."

I barely even felt my wings move, such was the extent of my newfound strength. I hurled myself up the wall, my fangs directed at his neck. One arm shot out automatically to clasp his dark hair, and I drew him to me.

"Ame!" Sabine's snarl came again.

Still gripping a writhing Beltran, I turned to find her crouched over a female Vampire, clutching the bitch's neck in her teeth. Her eyes were fixed on the open space beyond the wall, where three more Vampires had appeared. A further three scurried like rats from the shadows as Sabine clamped down on her victim's throat and a fountain of blood sprayed over her.

Even with my hand on his throat, Beltran coughed, "You're outnumbered, Cruxim."

"It has ever been the case." I could smell his blood, taste it. It was sweet vengeance with a hatred chaser. But as I kicked out to take one of the advancing monsters off the wall, I was distracted by a shout from the street below.

"NOW!" a voice bellowed, its insistence interrupted by a terrible roar that could only be Sabine.

Balanced on the wall as I was, I spun and lost my footing, pulling Beltran to the ground with me and taking his punch to my brow as I fell. Blood stung my eye. I scratched at his face with my nails, fighting against his strength to pin him down long enough. It would take just minutes for me to drain the blood, the mirth, the sheer cockiness right out of him out through his jugular.

Yet all around me the wailing continued. I stopped in my task and raised my head. Through the red haze, I saw Sabine inching backward. The hair on her back was raised in hackles and her high-pitched caterwaul was one of terror. No Vampire could bring on that fear in her, I knew. Then a great net, gleaming silver in the moonlight, descended upon her. One of her forepaws was quickly caught in it, and the more she tore at it, the more entangled she became.

"Sabine!" After delivering another a punch to Beltran's head, I climbed off him and swooped to her aid.

Beltran, ever a coward, climbed groggily to his feet and spun his black cloak around him like a pair of dark wings. A bat, he wheeled off into the night, screeching his mockery. There was nothing I could do but curse and turn to freeing Sabine.

Tearing at the net with my teeth and hands had no effect. It was of woven silver fiber, a rope of some supple metal, and even with some of my strength recovered, I could not break it. Blinded with blood, I swung violently, seeking the net's owner, and then heard the swoosh of another net cast about my own shoulders.

"Excellent work," a voice boomed from the shadows.

"We shall have our friend from the tower too."

A man stepped forward and shot a dart from a blowgun into Sabine's haunches. As she collapsed in a bundle of fur and claws in the dirt, I recognized our assailant.

Dr. Claus Gandler.

SEVEN

I came to sometime later, to a jogging sensation.

"Hurry! It's wearing off."

Despite wanting to strike out, I found myself too groggy and weak. Obviously, whatever they had dosed Sabine with had also poisoned me. The faint scent of sweat and carbolic soap filled my nostrils. I had been flung over someone's shoulder. A sound behind drew my attention to another man—a colossus who jogged along behind us with Sabine's inert body draped over his shoulders like a fur stole. Her head lolled with every bounce, and even her tail was motionless. I was gripped with a sudden panic that she was dead. Ahead, I saw a waiting coach, the driver cloaked in black. Then everything went dark again, a blackness interrupted only by incessant screams.

Sometime later, when my eyes opened upon moonlight, I knew I must have slept for an entire day. My body seemed intact and unharmed, although my shirt and coat were gone, leaving my wings exposed. The ground beneath me was cold, and I momentarily feared I had been returned to the cell in my tower. Then I felt the tug of motion beneath me as my weight shifted and realized I was on a wagon, in a sturdy cage on a wagon. To my left was another cage in which Sabine lay stretched out, her tongue lolling from her mouth.

I rushed to the bars close to her cage and stretched my hand toward her. "Sabine," I whispered. But I could not reach her.

Her chest rose and fell, and after some minutes, I saw the twitch of a paw. She groaned and swatted the air again. Then she rolled over and groggily lifted her head.

"You're alive!" The screams of the night before must have been nothing more than a bad dream. "Sabine, you should never have tried to help me. There were too many."

She yawned and tried to stretch her legs but, still unsteady from the sedative, stumbled and lay down again, giving her paw a lick to still it.

"They were not the problem." Her eyes fixed on the bars that contained her.

I lowered my voice even further, beyond a whisper. "Does he have it? The anchorstone?"

She growled gently in her throat. "If he did, I would already be dead." Padding to the bars, she eyed them cautiously, as if looking for weaknesses. Gaily painted wagons, many covered with canvas, surrounded us in a circle.

"Sabine, I thought of you the whole time: whether you would look for me, what you must have thought."

"Right now, I think we need to get out of here." She began to pace, her anger rippling in the small space like the muscles contained beneath her shimmering coat.

"It's no use. I've already tried. They're sound. Reinforced iron and as impenetrable as the bars of my tower."

"Your tower?"

I nodded. "Where I was imprisoned ... in Sezanne. Did

you think I had simply left?"

"I have searched for you for so long." Her voice was low. "I forgot what to think."

"How did you find me? I have hoped for so long that you might, that you cared enough to look."

"I have never given up looking. But it was not you I was watching last night. It was Gandler. If eternity has taught me anything, it is that it pays to keep a watchful eye on your enemies. As it turns out, he led me to my love."

"I am sorry, Sabine. So sorry about our last parting. For four decades, I have longed to make it right."

"What is four decades to ones such as us?" She rubbed against the bars, and her words were resonant with purrs. "You shall have eternity to make it up to me, but I am sorry too." I saw desire and playfulness sparkle in her eyes as she looked over at me. Then her features darkened with concern. "Your wings." She nodded at the tatty, battered white feathers.

"They'll grow strong again with use." I shrugged, wishing I had some way to hide them.

"You told me once why you feared him: eternity in a cage. He came to the tower. Told me he was a collector."

"He would say that."

"He had Joslyn's book. A gift I gave her. An illuminated incunabulum of mythological beasts."

Sabine raised her eyebrows at that and continued to prowl. "How many of them were myths?"

"Possibly none."

"Then you have your answer. He is a collector, Ame. Claus Gandler runs a freakshow."

"You might consider mindin' your manners," hissed a high-pitched, Irish-accented voice. The flap of a covered wagon next to me was rolled up a little to reveal a creature hulking in the corner of the cage. "Might be pertinent to mind who you go callin' a freak."

"Hush, Seamus. Take a look at the lad. He 'as some kind of wings sproutin' from his back." A hand set about rolling the canvas up a little more, until I could make out that the creature slouched in the corner was a man ... or rather two men.

Two heads, near identical in appearance, rose from one body, and an extra arm dangled uselessly on the left-hand side.

"Better'n having a second head sproutin' from his shoulders, I daresay, Sinbad."

"Or a lion sproutin' from her tits." Twin guffaws followed, and a hand shot out from between the bars to point at Sabine.

The man who had spoken first, Seamus, seemed most possessed of the torso, which was emaciated and filthy. I was surprised I hadn't smelled them first, although their wagon was downwind.

Sabine rolled her eyes and sniffed. Open hostility glittered in her stare.

"So what're you? Some kind of archangel?" The second twin, Sinbad his brother had called him, asked.

"No. A freak," I answered. "Just like you."

"Like us?" Seamus pointed to his brother.

"Yes. Like the two of you."

"Oh, that's where you're wrong. You see, we're not freaks. The only freak here is that fecking doctor, or so he calls himself. Pervert would be more appropriate. The rest of us, why we're jest unique. Ain't that right, Seamus?"

Seamus nodded until the two heads set to bobbing in unison.

I looked away, back to where Sabine stood, her lips curling in disgust, her tail charged with a potent energy.

"Freaks or no freaks, why are we here? What does he want with us?"

Seamus laughed again. "Welcome to the circus. He makes

coin off us. Exhibits us. If we're lucky."

"Roll up, roll up! Come see the unuuuusal, the unnnnnique, the peculiarities of nature. It's iiiiiincredible, un-be-lieve-able," Sinbad picked up immediately where his twin had left off. "The two-headed man! The woman so fat she eats three suckling pigs a day! The wolfman who tears men apart! The gigantor, able to lift a horse with a single hand. Roll up. Roll up!"

"Gandler just got two more acts," agreed his brother. "I wonder what he'll call you two?"

"The fallen angel? The whore of the pride?" Sinbad suggested.

I flew at the cage, my intensity forcing the single torso to shuffle back from the bars. "You might consider minding your manners," I snarled.

"Might," Sinbad said. "Except it looks like Gandler's got himself some pussy." The two of them broke into manic laughter.

"Ignore them. Pair of stupid Irishmen. Two heads and they couldn't rustle up half a goddamn brain between them," another voice interrupted from a wagon opposite.

"Catwoman meet wolfman," Seamus heckled.

"Shut your mouth, idiot," came the man's response. "We're in company. You could have given them a pleasant welcome." A hair-covered hand crept out and began to roll up the canvas from the inside.

"Welcome, welcome," Seamus said. "Welcome to hell. Come right in, the water's warm, and the fecking werewolf's awake."

"How many times do I have to tell you and your other imbecile head that I'm not a werewolf?"

Thick dark hair covered the man from head to toe, sprouting even from the palms of his hands. His eyes, which peered out from behind a matted mop of hair, were a dark, intelligent brown. "I'm Theron, the wolfman. Pleased to make your acquaintance. What are those things anyway?" He gestured towards my back. "Wings?"

I shrugged and tried to flatten them a little. I wasn't used to being seen, not like this, and I knew that my time spent in the tower must have made me a pitiful sight.

"You some kind of angel or something?"

I shrugged again.

"Not much of a talker."

I met that with another shrug.

"What about her?" Theron pointed to Sabine.

"I am a Sphinx," she said, her voice haughty.

"Hah." Theron sounded skeptical, but there was no denying that Sabine was intriguing.

"Looks like Gandler finally got himself a real one," Theron said and pushed the hair out of his eyes. "Or two." Then he pulled the canvas back down and went quiet.

Afterward, once the others had retreated behind their covered cages, I mentally reprimanded myself for not being friendlier to him. I wanted to know more about what Gandler might have had in store for us, find the chink in his armor that might enable us to escape. He might have been able to help me with that. I swore under my breath.

Sabine was silent, continuing her pacing.

"Do not worry." I soothed her. "It is as you say: he does not have the stone."

"Ame." Her voice was soft and low, and she turned her eyes full on me for the first time and stopped pacing. "They tortured you, didn't they?"

I nodded. "Yes, but there was no torture like missing you."

A brief smile danced at the corner of her mouth. "I am afraid, Ame."

I reached out through the bars again, longing to touch her face, to draw her to me and comfort her like the old days. "It is okay. I will watch over you. Protect you."

"You cannot reach me. No one can reach me. And every day I will be gone. Stone."

Sudden terror tore at my heart. "Sabine, what will happen ... if ... if they destroy your body?"

She laughed, but it was a terrible sound. "Nothing. Every day my body will vanish at sunrise, my spirit will fly to my anchorstone. At sunset, my body will reappear, whole and complete, in the exact spot from whence my spirit flew at sunrise. Oh, I will ache with it all, feel it all, but even if they should cut me into a thousand pieces by nightfall, I will reappear whole, intact, the next day, as if the anchorstone has created me anew."

I remembered how quickly she had always seemed to heal, and how long the days had seemed without her. "You can't appear elsewhere?" It was a futile question. I already knew the answer.

"No. By day, my spirit is bound in the anchorstone, but when it returns, it is to the place where my body vanished. We may choose a new anchorstone if we feel we are in danger, and many times have I done so since Gandler began to persecute me, but we must do that by night and in person. Only the destruction of my chosen anchorstone will kill me. The torture..." She trailed off.

I bowed my head, knowing her terror, the curse of immortality, and we fell to silence.

"How did you know?" I asked her eventually, jostling her out of her silent worry. "About the girl—that it wasn't Joslyn? That she was human? Had I drank from her it might have meant my death."

Sabine fixed me with a sad look and her eyes turned darker for a second. Then she looked away. "I didn't."

"Then why did you stop me?"

It was dark, but I could see the green shine of her irises as she whispered, "Jealousy."

Our silence was soon interrupted by a metallic rattle of

the bars.

"Look lively," came a voice out of the darkness. A light bobbed close to the ground, and a metal pannikin clattered against the bars of the cage next to mine. "Dinnertime."

"Sinbad, wake up. The fecking dwarf's here," I heard Seamus say.

The small, stunted figure stopped at the twins' cage and shoved through a mash of barley and ground meat. Then he approached my wagon and stopped, staring up at me in fascination.

"An angel, is it? Well, what on earth do you eat?"

A scar ran across the dwarf's lower lip, turning it down at the corner and slurring his speech a little. If not for that, he might have been handsome once, even despite his short stature and his scowl.

"Little people."

He gazed at me a minute and then smirked. "Oh, we have a jester, do we? Think it's amusing to make fun of my condition?" He tore a dagger from the belt that held up his too-big britches and jabbed it through the bars, trying to slice at my legs.

I stepped back. "I'll have whatever that gruel is you're serving up. Unless you happen to have a Vampire on hand."

"Vampire!" the dwarf hissed. "I'd have sooner seen the last of their kind."

"Then we have something in common, my friend."

"Call me that again and I'll stick you with this while you're asleep."

"Oh aye, he ain't no man's friend, this smug little devil," called out Seamus.

"Quiet!" The dwarf's reprimand was booming. "Or I'll have both ugly heads off your shoulders, you inbred pair. And you." He gestured toward me with the knife. "I'd suggest you keep a civil tongue in your head or I'll cut it out. I'd like to see you talk to your little pussycat here without it ... or maybe it's her tongue I'll cut out."

"Try it." Sabine strolled to the bars and issued a growl that seemed obscene coming from her feminine lips. "Meat for me, thank you." She glanced in my direction. "He was joking. But a few pounds of fat little midget ought to fill the hole in my belly."

"You'll have another hole there if you're not careful."

Sabine just yawned.

"Kettle, you're being tiresome again, it seems." The wolfman rolled up the canvas and beckoned the dwarf over. "Apologize to our new guests, Kettle, and explain to them how it is that you came to have your head so far up Gandler's arse that you're allowed to waddle around acting like you're ten foot tall and as normal as Tuesday."

"The good doctor sat down on him one day, I think," Seamus chimed in again. "His head's been up his arse ever since."

"That's enough!" Another voice from the far side of the circle interrupted. "I've been awaiting my supper all day and you're keeping it from me. Come to Trudie, Kettle. Come, little Kettle. Come feed Mama," the voice wheedled. "I'll not make fun of your size." The voice was a rich baritone and the words were followed by a wheeze, the cause of which became apparent when the dwarf threw off the covering of a huge wagon to the right. A mountain of woman lay sprawled on her back, her enormous legs spread by the rivulets of human flesh that puddled at her every joint.

"I'll have to come back for you, Trudie. The pigs haven't finished with the slop buckets yet."

Trudie, the fat lady, hauled her wobbling torso up on arms as thick as pillars and glared at him. "One day, Dwarf, I just might sit on you, too."

"Silence!" Kettle screamed. "Or I'll have the lot of you sent to Gandler's tent to scream along with that girl."

Everyone quieted, digesting the dwarf's threat.

"What girl?" I dared ask.

"New girl," Theron the wolfman answered. "Gandler found her wandering in a village, half dead, terrified, bite marks to her neck. She's one of them all right."

A memory of piercing blue eyes and a neck pale as a swan's tugged at my mind. "What does she look like?"

"Haunted," Sinbad said. "Probably quite beautiful once. Fair, with blue eyes. Just how Gandler likes them. Good thing she's already dead."

"Half dead," his brother corrected him. "Those screams last night suggested some life left in her."

"The screams? They were real?"

"As daylight. And if she's not dead tonight, you'll probably hear more."

I shook the bars of the cage furiously and the dwarf turned to me with a scowl.

"What is he doing to her?"

"He's a doctor, isn't he? He's operating."

EIGHT

It was evening before we truly discovered what Seamus had meant. The gigantor came for Sabine as soon as she reappeared in her cage.

Karl was half man, half giant. Built like a berserker, he appeared as dull-witted as he was enormous—a solid, bull-headed thug of a man with a jaw so sharp it could slice ham.

Dr. Gandler accompanied him. "Get her out," he commanded, and unlocked the door to Sabine's cage.

She pounced immediately, taking Karl by surprise, but his burly arms grappled with her, ignoring her swiping claws. Grabbing her hair, he yanked her head back and tweaked one of her nipples with the other hand.

Sabine let out a scream and made to bear down on his forearm with her teeth, but he let go of her breast and enclosed most of her throat, crushing down upon her windpipe until she went limp.

I pummeled wildly out through the bars of my cage in my struggle to reach her.

"Rest, Seraphim," Gandler told me gruffly as Karl flung

her over his shoulder and began to lope toward a tent at the other end of the camp. "I'll take good care of her."

Hours passed before Karl returned, but the body that lay over his shoulders was not Sabine's. The dwarf, an incongruous sight alongside his hulking companion, unlocked the door and Karl placed the slim white body of a girl on the floor of Sabine's cage. Wearing little but a bloodstained white gown, her body gleamed in the moonlight. Her neck was twisted awkwardly, but I would have known it anywhere. It hurt to look at it, to see it marred by the scars of my enemies.

The girl roused several hours later with a soft moan and half sat up, weeping.

"Hush," I whispered to her, and she righted herself and crept closer to the bars. A bandage covered her right eye and the other wandered, trying to locate my voice. When she saw me, her mouth formed a perfect O.

"You," she choked out. "You did this to me!"

"Me?" My wings flapped in involuntarily indignation. "No. My enemies did this to you. I could have saved you, remember. Could have stopped them."

"They ... they ..." Her sobs started again in earnest. "They stopped me one day as I approached the tower. It was late, nearly sunset by the time I left the village. I knew I shouldn't have ... it was too late. Too dangerous. But I had been thinking about what you said. About doing something about them. Ever since my uncle—"

"They killed him, didn't they?" All along I had known it.

She nodded. "Perhaps if I set you free, I thought," she continued. "You could rid the village of them, or at least be gone with them. I know they came for you." She put a hand to the bandage on her head.

"But the monsters found you first?" My heart thudded in my chest with what I at first thought was empathy but then recognized for what it truly was: my blood screaming for hers. Innocent she may once have been, but she was now a Vampire, and my very veins wanted her. "They turned you?"

She nodded again. "They would have turned him too—my uncle, I mean—had they not been discovered while his body was still warm. So many..." She shuddered. "So many have they taken."

I sat, pulling my knees up to my chest. Anger mingled with my bloodlust. "What is your name?"

"Danette." She put her head in her hands. "Danette was my name."

In the moonlight, I could make out a dark snake of fluid seeping out around where she sat. The thought of what he had done to her chilled me.

"How did Gandler find you?"

"The Vampire who found me outside the tower ... he was so quick. So strong. I ... I."

My voice was thick with loathing. "He is Beltran," I said. "A horror. You could not have escaped him. One day, I will avenge you."

"He took me to a house in Vincennes, an evil place. There were so many of them."

I could see the silvery hairs on her pale arm standing up in the moonlight and she rubbed at them. "They kept me there, chained, for a day or two, draining all of the blood from me. Each time it was like..."

I nodded. I knew the sharp yet sweet pain of it, the shuddering release, the intoxicating coldness, and the terror. I had seen the look of it so many times. "You do not have to explain that to me," I told her.

"Can you do it?" Her uncovered left eye looked huge, a well of sorrow in the mercurial light. "Turn me back? Or make me what you are?"

I shook my head. "I am not your salvation."

"Then I am damned."

I looked away, out over the covered caravans. *You are all*

damned, I thought. *Perhaps we all are.*

"Damned for all eternity, or at least until he dies." She began to weep again.

For a minute, I thought she meant Beltran, but then I remembered Gandler was human—if one could call him that. Judging by the state of the girl's body, Gandler was a monster in mortal form. The true freak amidst his freakshow.

"Gandler and his men attacked the coven. Set the coven house afire. I had thought the Vampires might leave me there, but the others set me free to fight. I was too weak, too weak to fend them off. Karl, of course..." Her hands flew to her throat and I remembered her silent prayers in the tower, the way her lips had moved slowly sometimes when she looked at me. She had been a pious girl. A good girl, and yet ... I said nothing, just nodded, knowing that I myself had struggled under the enormous man's bulk.

"And the others fled. I was just a pawn to them. Just another plaything. They have houses everywhere, it seems."

"Yes, they are like rats. Vermin. Always multiplying." I hung my head. "It is my failure."

Ignoring my shame, she continued. "Gandler seemed so proud of himself. He kept mumbling something about finally having caught one again."

I motioned towards the blood seeping from the bandage around her eye. "What did he do to you?"

She closed her eye a minute and then reached up and removed the bandage.

The bloody hollow of her eye socket, the vacant darkness where her right eye should have been, startled me.

"He wanted to know how our eyesight is so good." Picking up the bandage, she began to carefully wind it back around her crown and over her missing eye. "And he took blood. So much blood. It near drained me. And then..." A sob choked her. "I suppose it was no good to me anyway, what else he took." She tugged at the hem of the gown, and I saw her good eye linger on the trail of blood. "Do ... do ... can Vampires have children?" she asked suddenly.

I remembered then that she was just a girl, little more than a child.

"No," I whispered hoarsely, understanding what she meant. "Not in that way."

"Good." Sitting back, she leaned her head against the cage and wailed.

Hours later, when exhaustion finally silenced Danette, I paced my cage. Once more, I had failed. What fate might have befallen Sabine? The same fate that ruined this child? What a monster to take the eye, the looks—the womb!— of this child whose mortality had already been stolen from her. And Danette was just a girl he did not know. A stranger. He hated Sabine. What atrocity might he foist upon her?

Finally, just before daybreak, Karl and the dwarf returned. After unlocking the door, the dwarf grabbed Danette by the ankle and dragged her out of the cage. The movement of her body trailed her blood across the floor and it sickened me how much I craved it so. Had I been able to escape my own cage right at that moment, I would have ended it for Danette then, gladly. She and the world would be better for it.

Rope bound Sabine's paws together and a trickle of blood ran from the corner of her gagged mouth. Her body was still, only her eyes moving as Karl threw her off his shoulder and down into the cage with a thump.

The gigantor picked up Danette, who was still weak and disoriented. "Come on," he told the girl. "Your turn again. Seems the boss has quite an appetite today."

Before he clanged the cage door shut, he reached over and roughly tore off Sabine's gag. "Rrrow," he taunted.

The roar that followed was deafening, but when Sabine

opened her mouth to emit it, I saw that all of her teeth had been removed, and once more I vowed revenge on these freaks and their master torturer.

When Sabine's strength returned and she finally broke free of her bindings, I discovered he had taken her claws too. The look on her face told me she did not want to discuss it. How I wished I could hold her in my arms again. Even despite the bars, the rising sun would have soon made it impossible. Within the half-hour, Sabine vanished into thin air. Only then did I lie down and sleep.

When I awoke at sunset, I saw that Sabine's words were true. As soon as the moon rose, her spirit had returned from the anchorstone and she had sprung from the dirty floor of her cage as if newly arisen. I saw the gleam of her ivory teeth as she paced, and she unsheathed her claws to scratch at the straw of the cage. As good as new, but her eyes were harder and her nostrils flared with unspoken rage. Slinking as close to the bars as she could, her sinuous body rubbed against them as she whispered, "We must escape from here, Ame."

I knew it myself. I had spent much of the previous night pondering how we might do so.

"They will come again to torture me by night. Every night. He will not rest until I am torn limb from limb. Until he breaks me and I reveal the stone's location just to make it stop." She paced.

No doubt, the frustration of Sabine's daily resurrection would goad the man further.

Part of me wished I'd had the luxury of breaking back in the tower, that I could have revealed all to my torturers to end the agony, but there was nothing I could admit to, nothing I could reveal under torture that would enable them to kill me; not unless I had taken one of them down with me.

I balled my hands into fists and struck at the bars. Damn them! I'd had enough of bars to last a lifetime. How could I protect her from behind this iron?

All of a sudden, I heard the crack of a whip, and the wagon behind me began to pull away.

"Eh oh! We're on the roll, Seamus me lad."

"Looks that way, it does, Sinbad."

"Shut your stupid heads." Kettle's voice rang out from the darkness. "Stop standing around gandering or I'll set Trudie on you," the dwarf instructed a team of unkempt, slack-jawed men who stepped from the shadows. One of them held a buggy whip and harnesses, and the others led a team of small, wiry ponies, which they set about harnessing to each wagon.

"We're on the move," I whispered to Sabine. "Perhaps they will not come for you tonight after all."

"Perhaps," was all she said, her eyes fixed on the dwarf.

"Where are they taking us?" I called out to Kettle as my wagon began lurching away from Sabine's.

"Another town. Gandler's got some new prize pigs for folks to gawk at. Better start thinking about your act, Feathers."

I was relieved to see that he was hitching a pony to Sabine's wagon too. For now, she was at least remaining with me.

When Kettle strode off to hook up Theron's wagon, I turned back to Sabine. "I wonder why they're moving us by night and not by day."

Sabine lay in a corner of her wagon and rolled half onto her back in that lazy way cat's have. Her eyes were on the ceiling and the stars beyond, the canvas having been peeled back to attach the harness. "Perhaps they're afraid the girl's Vampire friends might seek retribution."

"I doubt it. He turned her just to spite me. But if Beltran learned I were here, perhaps he might come." I slumped against the bars. The lumbering movement was strangely comforting, as was the thought that at least we were going somewhere. Out of the inky blackness, another wagon lurched up close to mine, and I noticed Theron crouched in the corner.

"We move," he said. "I hope you're ready for the show."

"Where is he taking us?"

"On the road. Plenty of people will pay for a look at you two, although most will wonder how he did it. How the great scientist managed to sew the face and breasts of a woman on a wild beast. How he attached wings to a grown man. Just as they wonder whether my mother had relations with a wolf pack." He laughed, a wild sound but not quite a howl. "I'd wonder how he did it myself, except that I sense he did not."

His eyes raked me intently. "Oh, it is easy enough to keep Trudie as she is. So easy to enable her, to fatten her up. She's not the brightest of women, but I pity her. Those two idiots"—he jabbed a thumb towards the Siamese twins and lowered his voice—"are naught but a frightening reminder of the dangers of incest. Some say their parents were brother and sister. But this"—he tugged at the matted beard that fell from his chin and pushed the hair back from his hirsute face—"this, he tells me, is a disease. Hypertrichosis, the good doctor calls it."

"I call it unfortunate."

"Yes," the wolfman agreed. "Most. But what do you call yourself?"

"Amedeo," I answered.

His grin gleamed in the moonlight and he cocked his head just like a dog. "Very well then. You are close-mouthed, Amedeo." He paused. "I trust that. And the feline?" He nodded to where Sabine's wagon lurched behind mine.

"Watch your tongue. Sabine is no animal."

Theron nodded. "Nor am I." He lowered his voice further

still. "What I want to know is what you two intend to do about it."

"About what?"

Theron spread his hairy hands at the procession of carts. "About this little sideshow. None of us has the strength to stop Karl. But you two ... it doesn't take a genius to recognize you're different. Stronger. Supernatural."

I did not know how to respond to that. Could this hairy stranger be trusted? Could any of them? It was too soon to tell.

"I saw her, you know. They took out her teeth. Removed her claws. And yet, here she is again. Unchanged. Leonine. Feminine. And wholly unnatural. And you? If they pluck out those feathers, what will happen?"

I stared straight ahead, watching the jostling rump of the pony in front of me. "I will not be able to fly."

The wolfman's eyebrows quirked up. "So it is true then?"

"Yes."

"Then Gandler's Circus has both angel and devil, and who shall win the battle for our poor mortal souls?"

"No abomination shall triumph over the Father of all creation." Even as I said it, it felt false. Already, Beltran and his abominations were terrorizing Europe, and my Father was an absent one who had long ago abandoned his son.

"And that pitiful, screaming girl," Theron asked, "what do you make of her?"

"An abomination," I answered. "Though one not of her own choosing."

"It is true then also that you feed on Vampires?"

"Yes."

"Hmmm," Theron said thoughtfully. "Then what, Archangel Amedeo, eats you?"

"Regrets," I answered. "Only regrets."

And the moon above our wagons seemed as large and blue and brimming as Joslyn's eyes once had.

NINE

At least there were no screams that night, only the constant creaking of the wagons and the intermittent jogging farts of the ponies. Sabine was quiet, brooding, and for a time I was too, considering Theron's words and how I might act upon them.

"When we reach our destination," I called out to him after a while, "how does he exhibit us? In the wagons? In chains? Or in a tent?"

"Sometimes all three. But we're heading for Provins this time, city of the greatest fairs Europe has known. My guess is that there is to be some sort of showmanship. Gandler is a man who likes to be admired. But above all else, he needs his curiosities to fund his research, not to mention to be its subjects. A good show ensures a fat purse."

"I know something of this Gandler," I admitted. "His research is into vampirism. Blood disorders."

"Yes." Theron nodded, and a flag of hair flopped into his eyes. He flicked it away from his face with one hand. "Hence the girl, the bloodletting."

"He seeks a cure for vampirism?" I found it hard to believe.

"I think not." Theron gripped the bars. "He seeks an injection, an easy way to exterminate them."

"Then we share the same vision: angel and devil."

"Do innocents suffer for your ambition, Angel?" His tone came harsh to my ear.

My lips formed the word "No," but then I thought of Joslyn, and of Danette lying wombless somewhere in the night, and the objection died on my tongue. "Not if I can help it," I said instead. With a scowl, I kicked the bars. The clang made the pony skitter off the path, and it kicked back until Kettle was upon us, running a baton down the side of the wagon and swearing at both Theron and me to get on the floor. He hit the dun pony that hauled the wolfman's wagon, to hurry it up, and it pulled away. We said no more to each other that night.

All of the next day, the procession stumbled on without a break until the affronting smell of us preceded our little band. The ponies were near to lame before Kettle ordered a stop and replaced some of them with others from a nearby village. These new beasts of burden were a mismatched lot, some oxen and a few plow horses, a few fit only for boiling into soup, but once they were harnessed, we continued.

"Could've organized some grub, couldn't he?" Sinbad complained loudly. "Even fecking Trudie will fade away to a Hungerkünstler at this rate."

"There's naught but bread until we get to Provins, I heard," said his brother, "and Kettle says that's for the horses."

"A chamber pot would be nice," Trudie's deep rumble spoke up.

"You can eat out of a chamber pot if you like, Madame Porcine." Sinbad again. "I prefer to eat real food."

"What do you know about food, Sinbad?" The fat lady's

tone was vicious. "You don't even have a stomach."

"I don't have a working hand either but I'll stick a knife in your gullet when I get out of here just the same, you tub of lard."

"Is there never to be any end of bickering?"

Theron's voice, I determined.

"Not until Provins," Sabine said calmly from the cart behind me. "Then I'll silence the lot of you, and the entire miserable crowd if I ever spring free from this cage."

"What about you, Feathers? Any threats you'd like to make for us poor disabled circus performers?" Seamus said.

"Only one. I'll have Gandler's head."

"'Tis an ugly old head indeed. I shouldn't think you'd be pleased with it."

"Mayhaps you can figure out how to graft it onto a tiger. Give your friend here a little playmate."

"I've have your heads too, if you insult her again."

"That's more like it, Feathers. Now you're learning. We all love each other in Gandler's Circus of Curiosities. You'll come to learn that. We especially love Kettle and that fecking hulk Karl what does all the boss's bidding. You be sure to love them specially well too now, if you ever get close to either of their heads, or their pricks."

"Thank you for your advice."

"We freaks got to stick together, don't we?"

The carts stopped again briefly at Joy-le-Chatel, little long enough for Kettle to shove some mashed grains and dry bread through the cages, and then the convoy of wagons was set in motion again, pushing on towards Provins. The gray, fortified walls could be seen in the distance just before the sunrise. Already, gaily colored banners fluttered from the battlements and the gates were busy with traders. Sabine's wagon had drawn up beside mine, and when she appeared as the sun sank, I could tell from her worried frown that she, like me, was wondering what the town held in store for us.

"A show, Theron says," I told her, and her curls bounced as she nodded.

"Let's hope it is not gladiatorial. And that it is quick."

"It will have to be at night. Gandler must know that." I tried to stretch my muscles. Days of stooping in the cage had given me a crooked neck.

Sabine sighed. "Yes. With luck, he means for the show to begin tonight. It might spare me another night of his perversions."

I wished again that I might touch her, stroke her hair just for moment. "I miss you," I said. "By day, when you are gone."

Sabine smiled, but her eyes remained sad. "What if ... what if he separates us by day? I could return to find you gone. Or ..." Her eyes rested on my sparsely feathered wings.

I knew what she was thinking.

"I couldn't bear to lose you again, Ame. Not now, when I have only just found you." She pushed her lovely face up to the bars.

"We need a place to meet. A place to go and wait if we should be separated again."

She smiled. "I know a place on the Rue Saint-Antoine, outside the Hotel du Sully."

I was curious about the choice, until she followed with, "There are two Sphinx statuettes outside."

She must have heard my sharp intake of breath because she looked up at me with a frown. I wondered how I had missed that in my searches for her on the night I was released from the tower.

"No," she answered, before I even asked the question. "I will not tell you where my anchorstone is. It is safer that way. Besides, you will know it when you find it."

My face must have betrayed my skepticism because she

added in barely a whisper, "You will know it with a kiss. But know this also: it is not in Paris."

"What is not in Paris?"

We both jumped, so stealthy was the dwarf's approach.

"Come on, time to plan our little event for tonight." He ran a wooden baton down the sides of the cage. "Everybody up! Gandler's paying you a visit. Look lively now."

"Is he bringing more to eat?" called Trudie. "I'm famished."

"No more'n these poor horses who've had to haul you here." Kettle was unsympathetic as he set about unharnessing the horses and hobbling them to enable them to graze. "And no funny business, not from any of you. It's been a while since I had to kneecap anyone." He swung the bat wildly. "But I'm still a dab hand at it."

Sabine answered with a snarl from deep in her chest, which elicited a ringing thwack of the baton against the bars of her cage. "Oh, he especially wants to speak to you."

"Well, tell him he better be quick." She extended her claws.

"Here he comes now."

The old man's black robe had been replaced by one of crimson, lined with cloth of gold. A top hat embroidered with a sun and moon sat atop his head. His eyes were as black and cruel as ever behind gold spectacles.

He approached and rapped at the bars of Sabine's cage with an ivory-tipped cane.

"Listen up, every one of you. Tonight will be an important occasion. I require each of you to be on your best behavior. Provins is a grand city, an old city, and a city where people relish the unusual." He paused. "I think you will all agree that you are, indeed, that." His obsidian eyes stared at each of us in turn, and I noticed that Theron's topaz ones were barely able to conceal his hatred of the man.

"Tonight, we have a pavilion outside the Grange aux

Dîmes for a gala opening," Gandler went on. "The two-headed man will start the show."

"We're two men with one body," grumbled Seamus. "Will you tell them that?"

"Of course not! Trudie, most magnificently fat of women, you shall have a room of your own. It seems my ... research ... is becoming costlier of late, so I have decided to, how shall we say, hire you out. Although I am sure you shall have many admirers but quite a few taking me up on my offer."

A gasp came from Trudie's wagon, and the axels shook as she wobbled herself up to a sitting position. "I won't do it."

"My dear woman, the question is not whether you will, but how you won't? What will you do? Run away?" Dr. Gandler's smile was truly cruel. "The rest of the act shall be more melodramatic. I shan't spoil the excitement for you, but know this, Wolfman, She-cat and Angel, should any one of you fail to obey my orders, my ... entertainments ... shall become increasingly inventive. I'm sure my audience will not be bothered should my she-lion lack tits and a tail, or my angel or wolfman, a prick."

"You wouldn't dare," Theron started, but Gandler held up one wrinkled hand.

"Try me. Karl will come at sunset, and the dwarf will bring your costumes."

"And Angel..."

I stared at him, not bothering to conceal my disgust.

"You shall fly."

The long day without Sabine was broken only by the distraction of watching Gandler's henchmen prepare for the circus. A young man, his face a mosaic of ugly scars, was mending a net, another polishing a helm. Somewhere, another employed a hammer and nails.

"So, Feathers." Theron had adopted the twins' nickname

for me, and it stung. I had thought him more civilized.

"Wolfman," I responded coldly.

"I hope you two intend to play by the rules tonight, since both of our pricks are at stake."

"There are rules?"

Theron laughed. "Only one."

"Escape."

"No. The opposite. How do you think he has Karl and Kettle do his bidding? I assure you it is not love alone. Hate is a more formidable master."

"Yes, and I am beginning to hate the two of them near as much as I hate Gandler."

"Don't." Theron padded over and took a drink from a bowl in the corner of his wagon, holding the bowl up to his mouth like a man, rather than lapping at it like a dog. "They do his bidding because he threatens them."

"How so?"

"Gandler has Karl's eighty-five-year-old mother locked in cell somewhere. Should Karl disobey him, or even displease him, he beats her."

"And Kettle?"

"Children."

"Kettle has children?"

"Yes. He was once an exhibit, like you and I, as was his wife, Kira—a tattooed lady the likes of which you have never seen. They tried to escape when the first babe was born, but Gandler caught them. He took the babe as punishment. The boy is already twice the height of his father. He travels with the camp, acts as Kettle's whipping boy should the dwarf step out of line. You may have noticed the scars."

"And the other children?"

"A girl. Born a dwarf like Kettle. Poor wee thing. Gandler threatened to use her in his acts unless Kettle does what is required of him, or to sell her to a brothel when she comes of age. But he also has her help him when he operates."

"And Kira?"

Theron dragged one hairy hand across his throat. "Gandler cut her throat. Some say she was pregnant with their third child."

"He is serious then, about the repercussions should Sabine or I try to escape."

"Deadly."

"Then I suppose the net is for me."

"Or for Sabine."

"Tell me"—I stared into his eyes, trying to gauge the measure of the man through the hair on his face—"what form do you think these entertainments tonight will take?"

"Mostly bad dramatics. Re-enactments from popular play or stories, or sections from scripture, but with a macabre or ridiculous bent. I lost count of the times I had to stalk and attack a contortionist who played Red Riding Hood." He paused. "She is dead now too. Once, for a private showing for a wealthy man, he wanted me to rape her. When I did not, after the act, Gandler strangled her right before me. She was fourteen years old; I loved her like a sister."

"This is why, isn't it? Why you are all so hateful to each other?"

"Yes. It does not pay to show any affection."

"Then I will not fail you. I will do as he bids in the pavilion."

"And I. But what if what he bids is abhorrent."

I shrugged. "Something tells me his retribution will be worse."

"Easy. Easy now, girl." Kettle coaxed the ring of thin wire into the cage, all the while talking to Sabine as if she were a beast he was trying to soothe.

I could tell by the gleam of her eyes that she wanted to leap from the cage and tear the dwarf's head off, but she just lay in the far corner, her tail twitching and her luminous eyes following him intently.

Earlier that day, I had been awoken by the clanking of chains as several of the wagons departed for the city. The sun was huge and red, sinking into the muted green landscape by the time our wagons began to move off for the gatehouse set between the city's enormous stone ramparts.

Sabine had not yet appeared, and it worried me. What if something had happened to her? What if Gandler had found her stone? I wondered whether there had been any truth in her comment about the Hotel du Sully. What if her anchorstone were there and Kettle had told his master what he had overheard? Just as I thought it, Sabine reappeared, and our wagons passed through the gates and on to the grassed lawn inside the ramparts.

Each wagon had been assigned a teamstar. Mine was just a boy. Lee, his name was. Sabine's was the other boy with the face full of scars.

"Has the circus come to Provins before?" I asked over the clop of the pony's feet as the boy led the wagon through the gates. He ignored me and spat on the cobblestones.

Inside, a flood of people had filled the streets, some carrying produce or other goods for market, some even herding geese or pigs. Around us, the air had been fetid with a thousand scents: cinnamon and spices, flowers, the tang of citrus and of curry, and underneath, the fragrance of skin and sweat, of sex and shit, that I had come to associate with humans. Over them, I had smelled a closer scent, an older scent: the rank tang of fear. At first, I had thought it came from Sabine, but then I'd realized the scent was Trudie's. Sabine was too proud to be afraid.

We had moved through the streets slowly, making for the grand pavilion. Lanterns illuminated the inside of a large black and orange tent and threw curious shadows on the outside that served to both elongate and obfuscate the acts inside. The rest of the wagons stood outside, all covered with canvas to hide the acts from prying eyes.

Even now, as Kettle did his best to loop the thin wire around her neck, Sabine remained calm. It struck me as odd. I had never seen her so subdued. She had no intention of making his job easy, but nor did she resist him, and when he finally slid the noose over her neck and jerked it tight, she stood and ambled over to him like a lamb. "Come, Kettle," she said, with a final look at me that seemed almost wistful. "Let us get this over with."

"Oh, this will never be over with," Kettle said.

I remembered what Theron had told me and this time heard not malice but sadness in the diminutive man's words.

"Not until we end it," I added under my breath.

"Sit tight, Feathers." All trace of sympathy vanished from Kettle's face. "I'll be back for you in a minute."

When he led her away, I felt my throat tighten. "Sabine!"

She turned her head to me but kept moving forward.

"I ... I ..." The words cooled on my tongue. Better to pretend I cared less.

She nodded, and I saw that she understood. With a curt nod, she said, "Amedeo," and then vanished from sight.

Some time later, Kettle reappeared, this time with Karl. A pair of steel manacles swung from one of Karl's gigantic forearms and on his shoulders rested a wooden cross.

"You'll need to put this on." Kettle tossed something in through the bars of my cage.

I strode over to it, curious. It was a crown of sticks, the ends sharpened to resemble thorns. It left me in little doubt as to the role I was to play.

"And these!" With a clank, the manacles Karl threw hit the floor of my cage. The rustle of silk followed them. "At least until we get you up on the cross."

I attached the manacles to my ankles, donned the black silk robe, and put up the hood, and then I let Karl pull me from the cage.

Closer to the big top, I could hear a voice booming above the cries of the crowd. We passed into a pavilion through a smaller tent. To my left, a small crowd had gathered around an alcove where Seamus and Sinbad sat on a blue velvet cushion, feeding each other grapes with their one good arm. The alcove opposite was covered with a thin veil of silk curtain. A cloud of people spilled out from beyond it, all laughing and pointing. Beyond the crowd, I could make out Trudie's ample bulk splayed out on cushions, and even through the curtain, I could tell she was naked short of the rouge that reddened her plump lips and cheeks. Wet gurgles occasionally broke through the laughter and leering. She was either sobbing or otherwise occupied. It seemed Gandler had underestimated her appeal. There were some men prepared to humiliate a woman like Trudie even further.

"Hurry." Karl shoved me toward the big top, where the ringmaster drowned out Trudie's mewling.

"Gambling, whoring, drinking," the voice bellowed. "And look at humankind's sins. Look what comes of a life of excess, of men fornicating with beasts. Behold the wolfman!" I heard the crowd gasp and hiss, and Karl pushed me up to stand behind a screen in the back of the arena.

Out front, I could make out Theron, crawling on hands and feet around the ring, snarling.

Karl stripped me of the silk robe and slashed at my chest with a small pruning knife. I flinched but it was not a deep gash, just designed to make me bleed. "Congratulations, Messiah. Tonight you get to play our Lord and savior. Listen to Gandler, and when he calls upon the savior of man, I'll drag you out. Here."

I collapsed suddenly under the weight of the wooden cross Karl dumped across my shoulders. "You'll need this."

"An abomination," Gandler's voice boomed out. I searched the arena for him until I located him on the pulpit, dressed in the robes of an archdeacon. "You have seen already the wickedness of sloth and lust in fat lady Trudie. In the aberration of two heads on one body, you see the shame of incest, and now, you see the disgusting, filthy punishments meted out when man and beast sin together. The wolfman, whose mother fornicated with a vile animal, and this, the repugnant she-beast whose father's repulsive sins created this monster."

The crowd screamed in indignation as Gandler said, "Reveal ... the femme-feline, the disgusting she-lion."

The crowd gasped again, and me along with them. How I wanted to tear Gandler's heart out for that. How dare this man, this monster, this torturer, lecture others with lies while he spent his nights performing evil?

From the other side of the stage, Sabine leaped from a black curtain with a growl. Her head held high, she stalked the arena, eyes glaring.

"See," Gandler started again. "See the evils committed in the world today. The horrors. The freaks. This I show to you in the name of order and of decency, so that we may weed out these vile sinners and tear them down. So that we, the good citizens of Provins, might send them down to hell."

By this time, the crowd was rabid with evangelism, their eyes fixed on Theron and Sabine. Both prowled the front rows, baring their teeth and acting, for all the world, like bloodthirsty beasts.

Gandler's voice dropped an octave. He spread his hands wide before him. "But, good people of Provins, there is salvation. There is repentance." He bowed his head. "For God so loved his people, his honorable, good and righteous believers—although sinners every one of them—that he gave his only son to redeem them."

I felt a prod in my ribs and the weight of Karl's makeshift sycamore cross hurt even more keenly. "Go," he said, pointing toward the arena. "Carry it out there."

"Naked?"

"As the day you were born, apart from this." He shoved the crown of thorns down on my head. It tore at my forehead and sent a trickle of blood into my eyes. "That is, if you were born, Feathers. How are angel freaks made?" He picked up the helm I had seen the boy polishing earlier that afternoon and put it on, taking up a javelin from the back of stage.

"Why don't you ask Gandler? He seems to be the authority on how freaks are made."

"Go!" Karl shoved me out into the ring, leaving me no choice but to struggle forward, the cross on my back.

Karl followed. Every few seconds, he jabbed me with the javelin until I stumbled into the center of the arena.

The cross obscured my wings at first, and the whistles and catcalls of the crowd rang in my ears. Over them, I heard Sabine's growl of rage, and I swung my head a little under the heavy wood to search her out.

Do nothing, my eyes implored her. Soon this will all be over.

When we reached the center of the arena, Karl yelled, "Stop!" and stabbed me with the javelin again until I collapsed to my knees. Taking up a wooden mallet and two wooden pegs strategically placed next to Gandler's podium, he gestured for me to place the cross down.

The crowd screamed out its awe and terror of Sabine and Theron and its approval of me—the Christ who would suffer to absolve the beasts—but I was under no illusion that Gandler would spare me the worst of his deprivations.

My eyes flew to Sabine again. Then I placed the cross on the floor. Karl scooped me up, as if I weighed no more than a child, and lay me down on top of the crucifix, one giant hairy hand holding my wrist as he took up the mallet and spikes.

You are used to this, I reminded myself as I felt the bite of the spike in the tender flesh of my palm. I remembered the cuts that marred my muscled chest, the earlier vivisection that had opened my chest and scarred a crucifix upon it. Torture is nothing to you. Nothing. This will soon be over.

Even so, it pained me more than I remembered. When the gigantor had driven his nails through both of my hands and hammered my feet to the vertical pole, he grunted and swung the cross upright, sliding it into a pre-prepared hole beneath the arena floor. The full weight of my body, sliding down the rough-hewn sycamore, tugged agonizingly at my impaled limbs, and I screamed out in pain. Through my tears of pain and the rivulets of blood from my forehead, I could make out Sabine. Her face was a mask of anguish as Karl jabbed her away with the tip of his javelin and then turned his attention back to me.

"Yes," Gandler's voice echoed around the ring, "the sins of others were absolved in the suffering of our Lord and savior Jesus Christ."

"Blasphemy!" I heard a woman yell. Her voice came strong and clear as a stream over the bleating of the crowd. "What blasphemy is this? The Lord our God will punish you for this atrocity."

Although my eyes were rolling in my head from the agony, the dragging, burning sensation of my own weight threatening to pull me into oblivion, I raised my head. The audience seemed unsure whether to applaud and cheer or scream in disgust. Most had their mouths open, their eyes fixed on me in religious fascination.

And then I saw her. I knew immediately that she was the woman who had spoken out. She was standing several rows back, her slender body half shadowed in the last row of seats that could be seen from the ring, but her face, skin, and hair were so radiant she would have glowed in pitch darkness. She was pale and fragile, but the silvery gleam of her hair coupled with eyes gray as an autumn moon gave her an ethereal appearance. Her lips trembled as she watched. For a moment, I thought I glimpsed the flutter of wings beneath the red cape that covered her shoulders. I shook my head on the cross and closed my eyes a moment. I must be seeing things. When I opened them, she was gone.

"No!" I cried out and struggled. The crowd screamed out its anguish with me.

"Although tortured and terrified," Gandler continued. "Christ prevailed on the cross."

To make the point, Karl stabbed the javelin in through my ribs, and I writhed with discomfort.

"Oh yes, he prevailed. He took on the sins of the world. The lusty, the lazy, the envious, the unbelievers, the thieves, the rapists, the murderers, all of the sins that result in freaks like these you have seen tonight, and he absolved them, and when he died on the cross..."

Karl gave me another sticking with the spear.

"...after three days, he rose again." Gandler nodded to Karl who stepped forward and held his hands up to me. Grabbing my wrists, he ignored my yelps of protest to wrench my body free of the wooden spikes that impaled it to the cross. A great rift of pain opened on my palms and blood spattered the canvas floor. My scream was a pure thing, a prayer. And the crowd silenced in terror.

Agony gripped me. My wings, which I had managed to keep folded in the center of my back, sprang forth as I leaped away from Karl and carried me up, up, up into the dome of the tent.

"And he ascended to heaven as the Holy Spirit, to forgive the small-minded, the weak, the repugnant sins of humanity," Gandler boomed.

The crowd rose from their seats. Cheers and whistles filled the pavilion as I flapped away from Karl, spattering him with droplets of my blood as I flew. I had soon reached the roof, where a net was strung, obviously designed to trap me should I have thoughts of escaping.

Looking down through the vibrant colors of the crowd, all on their feet clapping and cheering now, I fixed my eyes on the slow tic of Sabine's tail, the mesmerizing movement dulling my pain. When the pain subsided a little, I hovered there and searched the crowd again, but the woman with the hair as pale as gossamer was gone.

"Yes, God, Lord Jesus and his host of angels shall protect us all from the filth of these freaks. He shall cast them all down to hell." Gandler was really working himself up now. "Good people of Provins, give me your coin, so that I may continue God's work and detain these monsters of Satan until such time as the angels shall truly entreat our Lord Jesus Christ to come again and smite them all from this earth."

Kettle suddenly sprang from the curtains. He carried a pitchfork and net, the latter of which he threw over Sabine and Theron. Using the pitchfork, he prodded them both back toward the door. The crowd roared its approval and I flapped down to hover above Sabine, a subtle warning that I would brook no injury to her.

"Come, Feathers." Karl strode to a silken rope that dangled from the ceiling and the net above the ring dropped down onto me, tangling in my crown of thorns and my wings. Below me, Karl began gathering the edges to yank me towards him, but there was no need. I was long tired of this fiasco. I did not struggle. A night spent in the cage was preferable to Gandler's brand of miserable voyeurism.

TEN

They returned me to my cage, carefully concealed beneath the canvas cover, as soon as the crowd had filtered out to the stalls to buy rose candy and caramel apples, spun sugar, and toffees. But the cage next to mine remained empty. Well after midnight, I heard the clump of feet and saw Karl's hulking shape approaching through the mist. A white shape in his arms could only be the girl, Danette, and I shuddered. Despite our passivity in acting out Gandler's sick entertainments to his satisfaction, it seemed Sabine had still taken Danette's place on the operating table that night.

Damn him! We should have defied him, I thought, rubbing at the wounds on my palms. I would not make the same mistake again.

I had expected Karl to place the girl in Sabine's empty cage, but to my surprise, he opened my cage door and shoved Danette's weak body inside.

"You did well tonight, Feathers." Karl wiped his brow. "A present for you."

I scowled at him.

"Now, now, don't be ungrateful. I didn't even stick you hard," Karl sneered.

"Tell me, Karl, why do you do it? You have ten times the old man's strength, yet you do his bidding." I lowered my voice. "Once you killed Gandler, you could set her free."

"Shhh." Karl held one meaty finger up to his mouth and slammed the cage door shut, grinding the lock into place. "Don't talk like that." He paused then growled. "Don't be talking like I can trust you, Feathers. Just 'cause you got wings don't mean you're any better'n the rest of this lot. You'd sell me out just as quickly, no doubt. Now shut up. Eat your dinner."

I gazed around my cell for the clay bowl Karl or Kettle usually filled with gruel; then I understood what he meant.

In the opposite corner of the cage, Danette sat shivering. Her blonde hair was a mess of blood and her skin as pale as a wraith's. Even for one undead, she looked near transparent.

I shrank back from her in horror, but all the while my stomach growled for a taste of that pale flesh and my eyes remained fixed on the snake of blood seeping from her forehead.

"No," Danette said weakly. "Do not pull away." Her lips trembled and I could see the blood beat of her pulse at one corner of them. "Come to me. Come and hold me. Just once more, I would like to be held before I die. To be held, once more, by someone good."

Still, I pushed myself away from her, against the bars. This was another form of torture Gandler had prepared: for me to spend the night in this cage with her, longing for and pitying her.

"I am not the person you seek. Please, do not ask this of me. You are too close."

"I already asked it." She smiled weakly. "Did you think it was Gandler doing this to torture us both? No, this was my idea. I put it in his head by pretending to be terrified of you."

"You should be terrified of me." I gripped the bars, needing their strength to stop me from burying my face in her elegant neck. My hunger was debilitating. I closed my eyes, pressed my face up to the bars.

"Maybe once I was," Danette said. "But what could be more terrifying now than my own self? Look at me, Amedeo."

I lifted my eyes to her. She was indeed a pitiful creature. The only color in her face was her garish blood and the lurid swelling of the bruises that ringed her remaining eye. Slashes and pockmarks lined her arms, swelling to small red hillocks where the point of a scalpel blade or syringe had bled her. Her left arm had been amputated at the elbow, a new torture.

She laughed thinly. "Yes, you see what I have become. You must stop him, Amedeo. Don't you see what he is attempting to do? Nightly, he draws my blood and injects it into his own arm. So much blood. He tried to force me to bite him, to turn him, but I had not the strength. When I could not, he did this in rage." She waved the stump of her arm at me and groaned. "Imagine what he could be if he were immortal. The monstrosities he might commit."

"I would kill him!"

"Yes." Danette nodded. "But not if you are in here. And not if he has Sabine. You would not risk it. You love her."

She was right: I would not. And yet rage filled me brimful at the thought of one more of them, and one so evil as Dr. Gandler.

The night was broken by a scream. High-pitched and ringing, it echoed off the iron bars of the wagon and fled into the night.

Her huge sapphire eyes read the terror in mine. "Why do you think I wanted to come to you, Amedeo?"

"To warn me."

"Yes, there was that, but more than that. I came to you to die. I wanted you to feed on me. This earth is hell to me now. I can bear it no longer, and you are tired, tired and thin. Karl is strong, as strong as ten men. You could use the strength if you are to escape him. My blood will give you strength. If only I had set you free, so many months ago."

"Danette." My body cried out for even a single drop of Vampire blood.

"Go on. I see the look in your eye. The bloodlust. I know how you must want me. Nightly have I craved Kettle and Karl, Seamus and Sinbad, Trudie and Theron, and most of all Gandler himself. The thirst, this need for blood, it is unable to be slaked, insatiable. What a thing it is to feel so empty." Her bloodstained hand tugged at the gown at her throat, exposing her décolletage. I noticed her silver cross still dangled there, its brightness contrasting with the sizzling, blistered char of the skin beneath. She remained too pious to remove it, even though it caused her pain. "In the name of the Lord, I give you leave," she said, exposing more of her neck and chest.

"No!" I turned away from her so suddenly that I felt the swoosh of my wings as I spun. "I cannot. Danette, you have suffered so much. Too much. I cannot send you to hell. In Paris, in Montmartre, there is a physician named Monsieur LeRay. For a fee—"

Tears filled her eyes, and such a great sob burst forth from her that it stopped me. "And pray, tell me, how I will find this place? How will I first escape Gandler, and then, having done so, find the money to pay this physician the fee you speak of to send me to treat with Satan? You are right, Ame, I have suffered much. Too much. End my suffering." Her hands tugged at the gown again, and her eyes beseeched me. "Please," she whispered. "Please, hold me."

My breath escaped in a sigh of pain and relief and

anguish, and my knuckles released themselves from the bars. I did not tell her that her suffering would never end, that Satan had new tortures for her. She had been a good child who had been turned without consent. I still hoped I might be wrong. Turning, I flew to her and swept her into my arms, hugging her frail body to my chest.

"You are so warm." She snuggled against me like a kitten. "So very warm."

It will be eternally warm soon, my poor little one, I thought, but said nothing. Already I could feel the rhythm of her blood pulsing through her body, the sound of it calling to me to take her neck, that graceful swan neck, to my lips and to drain the life from her, to end the reign of the undead on earth one at a time, starting with this one nearest to me. To do my job.

"Do you know any scripture?" she asked, and I confessed that I knew only a smatter. After Gandler's little crucifixion, I did not care to be reminded of the Bible.

"Very well," Danette said. "I will recite."

"Danette." I embraced her closely, so close that I could almost taste her. My lips brushed her cheek just beneath her ruined eye, and my eagerness for her death shamed me—until I remembered that she had died weeks before. "There is no return from this."

"I will bless the Lord at all times: his praise shall continually be in my mouth." She started the Psalm, drawing her body even more tightly in, as if she might fold herself into me. "My soul shall make her boast in the Lord: the humble shall hear thereof, and be glad. O magnify the Lord with me, and let us exalt his name together." Her voice trembled only a little.

I put my lips to her marble-cold neck, pressed them against her jugular.

"I sought the Lord, and he heard me, and delivered me from all my fears." Danette's prayer rang out defiantly as my teeth grazed her neck. She stiffened when the point of them penetrated deep into the vein. I crushed her to me then, jerking her neck back by the silver chain, which came away in my hand, and pushing her down so I could drill my fangs in to their extremity. My movements become savage, innate, my mouth filled with her sweet, metallic warmth.

Danette gasped. "They looked unto him, and were lightened: and their faces were not ashamed." Her hand gripped me, beseeching me not to stop until I had finished what she had begged me to do. Her voice grew softer, but still she spoke, "This poor man cried, and the Lord heard him, and saved him out of all his troubles."

I could have wept for her, or for myself, but then I heard the poem of her, the gushing, rushing rhythm of her life flooding into me. Her heartbeat was like a heavenly choir alive in my blood as I sucked. She began to shudder, and as she reached weakly up to stroke my face, I saw that the sun was rising, as scarlet as the blood that coursed over my lips.

"The angel of the Lord encampeth round about them that fear him, and delivereth them." With a final quiver, she flung her hand out and pointed. In my peripheral vision, I caught a glimpse of a red cape and hair gleaming like quicksilver. I wrenched my mouth away just as the red sun rose above the horizon. And then, with a final shudder, Danette was nothing but ash. I clutched only her glistening cross, warm in my hand.

Thank God, I thought, for the sun. Sabine's screams will have ended for the night. What was left of the girl departed on a fresh breeze. I hunkered in the corner of my cell, on my knees, and sobbed my shame to the new day.

All day, my dreams were scattered, clouded with thoughts of Sabine, Danette, and the screams we had heard the night before. What fresh hell had Gandler prepared for her, and where was he keeping her? The night's rigors had exhausted me, but the day's dreams drained me almost as much. I jolted awake in the mid-afternoon, drenched and listless, the silver cross fastened around my neck.

"Heard you played your part well, Feathers," Sinbad called to me. "Best takings ever last night. But t'is morning, quite the kerfuffle, I hear. Seems that cat of yours escaped. Treacherous she-bitch. I'm surprised Gandler hasn't come to torture you over it yet."

"Heard Feathers was otherwise occupied last night, Sinbad," Seamus joined in. "What'd you do with that pretty little Vampire in the darkness? You might act like a gentleman in public, Feathers, but from what I heard you weren't no angel last night."

Sinbad laughed uproariously. "Wonder what old man Gandler would think of that atrocity. Or is that how you came about, Feathers? Mammy was an angel, Pappy was a devil? I bet that's it."

"Well, she's had her last now, hasn't she. A shame. Sinbad and me would have been happy to spend a night alone with her, wouldn't we? Afore you got to her, Feathers. They always say that two heads are better'n one, but I'm not sure how we could compete with Angel prick over 'ere. What is it, Feathers, made of solid gold and diamonds?"

"Bet it tasted like ambrosia and felt like a horde of heavenly cherubims humming in her cunny." They cackled like a pair of old fishwives.

I slammed myself into the bars of my cage so hard it nearly concussed me, but my hiss, and the fire in my eyes, was enough to frighten them into silence.

"Is it true?" I called out in the direction of Theron's covered wagon. But I was met with nothing but silence.

"Oh, you didn't hear?" Seamus's voice was slippery with satisfaction. "Theron made off with her too. Yes, your two little playmates let you get all tricked up like the Messiah on the cross and off they've gone to fornicate together. Seems angel prick's not all that potent after all, eh, Feathers? Or maybe she just prefers fur to feathers."

I didn't even bother to snarl this time. Let the imbeciles think what they would. There is nothing more stupid than arguing with stupidity.

"I heard she savaged one of Gandler's carnival men and that Theron put a trident through the other." Trudie sounded hopeful and a little breathy with the excitement of it all.

"But neither of them thought to come for you, Feathers, now did they?"

Impossible. Sabine would never betray me like that. My heart told me they were planning something, some way to free us all from Gandler's clutches. *Patience*, urged my mind. *She will get a message through.*

Gandler took no risks with my liberty. We remained in Provins, but no longer was I dragged from my cage to participate in Gandler's nightly amusements. Instead, a parade of pilgrims, disbelievers, and sightseers was pushed past my wagon all day and into the night, each clutching a Provins penny for the privilege of seeing me.

"They are stuck on," a small boy insisted, poking a hand in between the bars to try to snatch a feather.

"Our Lord God's heavenly host are mighty, glorious beings. This wretched monster cannot be one. How else would our Father allow him to remain in this cage?" a cowled monk declared.

"My, but 'e is 'ansome ain't 'e?" One of the women from the nearby market, a flower seller, came most days, tossing blooms in through the bars and blowing me kisses. "Imagine what 'e must've looked like in heaven. Ooo, I reckon 'e might take me there if I can figure out how to get 'im outta 'ere."

"Why don't you give him something useful then, you stupid bint," a fat farmer told her. "Stop throwing him roses and give the poor bastard a crowbar tomorrow."

"Everyone back, back away from the bars." Karl brandished a club. "If I see anyone throwing anything other than rotten produce in at this freak, I'll lock them up with him. Don't you idiots know he eats people?" He pulled a face at the crowd. They all took a step back.

"I thought he was an angel. Which is it? Is he mutant, myth, or man?"

"I'll go in wif 'im, mister," the flower seller shouted. "'E can eat me any day."

"Get back you stinking trollop." Karl walloped her broad backside with the back of the club. "And you"—he pointed at the farmer—"go take a bath. You stink, the lot of you."

"What happened to the others: the wolfman and the she-lion?" A small boy stared at Karl accusingly. "I paid coin to see an entire menagerie and the best you got is a man who's been tarred and feathered, a pig-fat whore. No offense, Mademoiselle," he said in the direction of Trudie, "and a man with two heads, and both of 'em ugly as three-day-old shit."

"Well, he ate the others, didn't he?" Karl insisted.

"Then I suggest you feed him more," said the farmer. "The poor thing's little more'n skin and bones."

"Don't worry, me love, on the morrow I'll bring you some sweet apples too." The flower seller blew me kisses as Karl herded them on. Behind her ample frame, I thought I caught a glimpse of silver hair.

"Wait," I cried and put a hand out through the bars, inwardly cursing myself for my brashness.

"Oh, sweet'eart," said the flower seller, thinking I meant her. She tried to clutch my hand, but Karl pushed her back again. "I'll be back, Sweet Angel. One day we shall fly away together."

The flower seller was true to her word; she came again the next day, but I turned my back and ignored her. "Moody today, me love." She threw in a bunch of flowering rosemary. That night, I buried my head in her bouquet and wept.

It had been ten days since Sabine and Theron had vanished, and still I had no sign of them.

"Man died from Theron's trident," Trudie told me. "And another from your lion's bite." I had given up paying any attention to Seamus and Sinbad, their company vexed me so, but Trudie's nightly appearances in the silken tent gave her access to the gossip. "Gandler brought out a new act last night: a woman who bleeds stigmata from her eyes, mouth and hands. Very beautiful, she is. More beautiful even than your Sabine."

"Probably just another fake," Sinbad sneered.

I ignored them.

"Sabine will return," I told Trudie. "Gandler has me watched day and night, but she will come for me."

"Don't be so sure, Feathers," Seamus said. "Gandler hung up half a lion's corpse and the body of a wolf from a gibbet post. Told the crowd they were killed trying to escape."

In the cage opposite, Trudie wobbled to a sitting position and began to rifle through the mound of food the procession of people had thrown into her cage.

"Theron was no werewolf. It was not him." I rolled my eyes.

"Aye. Nor was it her," Trudie agreed. "That was a male lion, up close. But it wouldn't do to tell people a lioness and a wolfman were prowling the city together."

I nodded. "This woman who weeps blood. What is her name?"

"Joslyn, he calls her." Trudie found half a moldy cake and stuffed it in her maw, then she continued, "But I call her bluff. She's beautiful, sure, but she has the unnatural look of that poor dead girl about her. I never see her by day. There's something not right about her. I hear tell she approached him too." Trudie swallowed down the lump of cake and followed it with half an apple. "I never heard of a woman who weighed less than three hundred pounds or weren't tattooed like a sailor wanting to join the circus."

"Joslyn," I repeated quietly to myself.

It cannot be her, I told myself. How would she know I was here? Then I reminded myself that half of France had probably heard of Gandler's angel at the freakshow in Provins. It was a wonder Beltran had not turned up. But surely Joslyn would not come. I had told her I never wanted to look on her face again, that if I did I would kill her, surely she would stay away. Unless...! I had a fleeting vision of Danette's face. No. No, it could not be. Had Beltran's ruse with the mortal girl been based on truth? Had Joslyn, like Danette, sought me out to die?

ELEVEN

Two nights later, I saw her for the first time in nearly two hundred and fifty years. Death had not wearied her. Her skin was luminous, and her eyes—those eyes—still shone bluer than the ocean.

It had surprised me, and the others, that Gandler had not set about torturing me following Sabine's escape. Perhaps he knew that my part in Danette's death was torture enough for me, or perhaps he was too busy hunting for Sabine to care. But there was no torture he could devise that would be as painful as seeing her face after so long. She came for me in the early evening. The bustle of the covered markets had died down, and the night was still and warm and so quiet that I could hear the crickets busy in the fields beyond Provins' walls. Oh, what I would give to be out there, flying above the fields under the bone-white moon, away from Joslyn, away from all of this.

It was two weeks since Sabine and Theron had vanished, and no word or sign had come from either of them. Kettle, too, had disappeared. Trudie said he was being punished for Sabine's escape. Every day, I looked for something that might provide some clue as to Sabine's whereabouts or her plans, but as each night segued into morning with no sign from her, I began to think perhaps the twins had been right, perhaps she had abandoned me. The only thing that prevented me from thinking Gandler had found her anchorstone and pounded it to gravel was that the man himself had not come to gloat over it.

The night Joslyn came, I got my answer.

The twins and Trudie were already in the tent, and Joslyn was dressed for the show. A white silk sheath with a cowl covered her lithe body. Cinched in by silver at the waist, it left her slender arms bare and free. Had it not been for the ethereal glow of her skin and the vermilion of her lips, she might have been an angel floating towards me—or a vision. My veins tingled, sensing the closeness of Vampire blood, but the man in me sensed her too. Yearning tugged at me, yearning for years so long past that it seemed as if all but the memory of them was dust.

"Joslyn?" I stood and grasped the bars of my cage.

She smiled a little and moved closer. "We must be quick." She pointed towards the big top.

"Yes, the stigmata."

The edge of her laugh could cut steel. "A pretty trick," she said. "But of course you know that. It is not a hard thing, to cry. To bleed."

"No," I said, awkwardly, remembering that night in the river, when my tears had come close to matching the stream's volume. "Joslyn, that night ... I ... It was a sin."

"Shhh," she said, one finger to her lips. "Not one so dark as this." She gestured to herself, her hand fluttering the white silk of her hood. Then she slid her fingers in through the cage.

The jolt of electricity when she touched me caused me to leap back, as if she had burned me, and her smile turned to a scowl that made her blue eyes gleam suddenly black as Gandler's. "This is how you would treat me—your rescuer?"

"My rescuer? Joslyn, you must not do this."

"I must." Her voice grew soft again, seductively so. "Ame, I must. For more than two hundred years, I have searched for you. And yet, ever, as soon as I grew close, they pulled me away. Beltran locked me in a coffin for half a century. Said you would kill me, kill us all, that I must stop this ceaseless, endless longing for things that were past. Mortal dreams that never were. But I knew." She put her other hand through the bars, both of them seeking mine, which trembled like a child's in hers. Slowly, Joslyn brought my scarred palms to her lips. My skin prickled at her touch, repulsed and stirred by the coolness of her kiss and the beat of her blood.

"He never told you?" I made to withdraw my hands, but she kept one clasped in her own.

"Told me what, *Meu angel de la guarda*?"

The words were sweet, but still each felt like a wound.

"Beltran never told you," I said again, wondrously. "The tower at Sezanne? You never knew?"

"You were at Sezanne?"

"For forty years. Held prisoner by the citizens of the village." I hung my head, but she caught my eye and her expression told me she had read something in it.

"Your wings..." She dropped my hand and made to stroke a wing feather, but could not reach it through the bars. "Gandler did not do this then?" she whispered. "He did not torture you? She lied to me."

"She?" I was confused. "Beltran knew I was in the tower. He came most nights to mock me. He never told you."

"And all the while I searched," she said slowly, sadly. "All the while..." She broke off and her face flushed with anger. "The jealousy. Oh, the cursed jealousy. He always hated you, would have done anything to keep me from you. But why would she lie to me?"

"She? She who?" The old expression leaped into my mind. *She's the cat's mother.* "Sabine...?" I breathed.

"She told me Gandler was a torturer. She came to me to save you. Said I was the only other being she could be sure would help to free you."

"She did not lie about that; here you are."

Joslyn pushed the hood from her head, and the wind took a strand of her long dark hair and blew it across her face. "Here I am," she said. "But he did not do this to you." She nodded to the scars that patchworked my chest.

"No, but he is a torturer all the same. He..." Danette's name stalled in my throat. "He tortured Sabine. He removed her teeth, her claws. Tormented her."

Sabine's softly spoken word that night in Paris, when I asked her why she had stopped me, sprang into my mind: Jealousy.

Had she brought Joslyn here to help free me, or in the hope that it might destroy her greatest rival? I shivered, and my wings flapped involuntarily in the darkness. "How did she find you?"

"She did not. She found Beltran."

I must have looked puzzled at that, because Joslyn cocked her head back at me slightly. "The coven houses in Paris. Sabine told me you were captured there. She came there looking for me, knowing Beltran must be there somewhere. She guessed he would know my whereabouts."

Anger thickened my blood. "Why do you stay with him?"

"Where else is there to go? I did not stay. Not at first. After the first deadened months, I crept away inside myself. I flew to Dubrovnik, hid myself like a monster. A bat, I crawled inside the walls of Lovrijenac Fortress and withered there. All the while, Beltran searched for me."

And all the while, I thought, *I did my best not to.* What had I done myself, those first hundred years without her, but wander in a daze, lost in a nightmare of killing and blood and need and duty? Each neck, every set of fangs, a reminder of what she had become. How many nights had I wished to put an end to it all until I had met Sabine?

"What did she tell you about Gandler?" I quickly changed the subject.

"He's a torturer. He caught you in Paris, when Beltran attacked you, and forced you both into his freakshow."

"Joslyn." My voice had a chill to it. "You must leave this place. Leave at once! She has not told you what he is. He knows what you are, knows this little act is not stigmata."

Her eyebrows shot up and she shook her head. "Ame, he does not know."

"Dr. Claus Gandler hunts Vampires," I told her. "He has devoted his life to it. He knows! You must fly. Now, Joslyn. Do not delay. You are in danger." I could have cursed Sabine for not telling her.

"No, Ame. It is you who is in danger, but I have come for you. We will be together."

Her voice had a singsong quality that made her delusion even more apparent.

"Joslyn"—I put a hand up to the silver cross—"the girl who once wore this, he found in the village. She was my jailer … until Beltran. Please…" I felt my throat constrict with anxiety for her, even after all these years apart. "Please. Leave this place. Leave me."

She shook her head, and her curls bounced wildly. "Never, Ame. I love you."

I had forgotten how stubborn she could be, and how frustrating. I made my gaze as cold as Gandler's eyes. "And yet I would kill you—in a breath. I would feast on you and send you to a fiery tomb!"

How I wished she would leave.

"This thing you want, my love you crave," I hissed. "It is impossible! My entire being screams for your blood. If these bars were not here"—I shook the reinforced steel with all my force until my teeth rattled—"I would destroy you. I would consume you."

"Then so be it."

The roar from the pavilion rang in my ears.

"I must go. I will return later." Joslyn pressed her lips up to the bars. "*El meu angel de la guarda*, vengeance is coming for you, and her teeth are bared." Putting her fangs briefly to her own wrist, she made the tiny weeping wounds that would double as stigmata. Then she pulled back and her fangs gleamed with blood. "I will need no fake tears tonight." Her last look at me was one of undiluted sorrow; it stung my very soul. "The sight of you in a cage is enough."

I watched her float away, a wisp of white silk in the darkness.

"A beauty, is she not?" The voice was low and came from my left. Trudie and the twins were already in the tent, and Gandler was making more good coin tonight, if the applause from the audience was anything to go by.

I sprang back from the bars, into the corner.

"The stigmata woman. I never saw such purity." The last word came out sardonically. Then a whisper, "Some say she is the Vampire Queen."

"She is not." I stepped forward again, recognizing the voice and relieved it was only Kettle. Yet still, he could not be seen. "Kettle?"

"Aye. Down here, Feathers."

I looked again. "Blast, Kettle. Where are you hiding?"

"Do not yell, Feathers, or you'll be the death of me."

"The death of you...?"

"Pssssssst!"

The hiss came somewhere beneath me. I squashed my face up against the bars and squinted down toward the ground. Something crawled there, squirming like a puppy on its belly, something small and toothless and disfigured.

"Kettle?" I asked again.

"Yes, it's me. Are you blind, man? Be thankful you've still got two eyes to see a man who lacks two legs. Now, I suppose instead of Kettle the midget, men'll call me Kettle the cripple and be done with it."

It was then that I saw what had happened to him.

"Just when you think a man can't get any shorter, Feathers." He grunted. Blisters of sweat beaded his lip. "I suppose I should be lucky that he took only my legs for letting your feline friend escape, and not my head."

"Kettle..." I stared at the blood-soaked bandages, the stumps that terminated above the knee. "I'm ... I'm sorry."

"What do you have to be sorry about?"

"Your legs. For your loss."

"Shhh." Kettle put a finger to his lips and rolled onto his back. A grunt of pain came from the ground near the wagon wheel as the exertion sent a further dark stain seeping through the bandage on his thigh.

"Listen up. Before Karl gets back," he whispered, propping himself awkwardly against the wagon. "There's a lad here, Lee, who's watching you night and day, aye and listening too."

"She is not a vamp—"

"Shhh! God's whiskers, Feathers! Don't interrupt me. Lee's my boy. A bastard. Gandler doesn't know it. The other was mine too. The scarred lad. Kellane his name is. Used to be a handsome lad, did Kel. Gandler'd never risk letting him watch you alone now. He's taken him somewhere. Won't tell me where. He's insurance. But Lee—"

"I know Gandler keeps Kellane so you'll do his bidding," I said. "I know he scarred him."

"Aye."

"And your daughter..."

"What about her? If you'd shut up for a minute and let me finish, you might find out." Kettle leaned back against the spokes. His breathing was labored. "Look at me, not even half a man, though I'm grateful I've still got the parts that count for that title at all, I suppose. Look at Trudie, more woman than any man can handle. Those fecking twins—pair of idiots. The boss'd take one head off, if it didn't deprive him of an income. All of us doing Gandler's bidding, but we don't see a glint of that coin do we? But that girl, that sweet girl..." Kettle paused and mopped his brow with the sleeve of his shirt.

I presumed he meant Danette, or maybe his daughter.

"He did that to my Kira, you know," Kettle continued. "Cut her throat. And he's threatened the same to Giselle. Sweet little Giselle. Poor wee lass never asked to be brought into this world looking like she does. Lord knows I feel the shame of it, but dwarf or no', she's mine. Cooped up in Gandler's tent helping him with those terrible tasks. And all this time. All this time..." Kettle's voice was choked with sobs. "I've never been a big man, Feathers—"

"Amedeo, Kettle."

"Well, I've never been a big man, Amedeo, and I know all can see that, but to be a coward—that is another kind of small." He put his head in his hands. "And look what it's done to them. My Kira, she were a bonnie lass, she were. Brave and big, strong as a sailor and with the ink and the mouth to match, but how I loved her. And she loved me. Bore me two fine babes, she did, small as Giselle might be. Bore them bravely, but me..."

The man was rambling now, sobbing his words so much that spittle followed them from his mouth.

"Calm, Kettle." I tried to soothe him. "Bravery and brashness are stablemates. You are alive—"

"Yes. And my Kira is dead. And I should of done this years ago when she was still here to see it."

"Done what?"

"Killed that evil bastard!" Kettle spat the words out.

"Kettle," I warned, "calm now. What is behind all this? Have you seen Sabine? Theron?"

"Seen them? I freed 'em. Would have freed you too, had Gandler not punished me." He began to dab at his eyes with his sleeve again. "Yes, I know how hated I was. Karl and Kettle. David and Goliath. The midget and the monstrosity. That's what they all thought. But I am not like Karl. I knew which side my bread was buttered on. Small man like myself, you either wield the stick or you prostrate yourself and prepare to be beat with it. But with a man like Gandler, the stick is not the problem. The problem, Feathers, is the carrot. And what sweet carrots he had to make me wield that stick for him."

He was rambling again and sobbing openly now. I wondered what he had taken to make him even this coherent through his pain.

"Kettle, come now, man. Tell me before we are interrupted. Where is Sabine? Why has she brought Joslyn here?"

"Sabine, yes. There are dungeons, you see. Secret passageways." Kettle grimaced with the pain of staying upright. "Beneath the city. Kira and I met there, you know. Many years ago. She was a sailor's daughter. Provins always had a thriving black market. Dealt mostly in contraband down there in the cellars. Women. And rum. And—"

"Kettle! For the love of all things holy!"

"I'm getting to it." He groaned again and licked his lips. "God's whiskers, man, you ever taken laudanum?"

I shook my head.

Kettle flinched. "Under the Grange aux Dime, the secret passages. Kira and I used to tryst there. After what Gandler did to Trudie, tricking her up like a whore, and then that girl... the things Giselle told me, how he tortured her. Cut out her womb, he did. And Sabine, what he did to her. All a reminder of what he might do to my Giselle if I didn't find the courage to stop him. But how could I, a man of my stature? Sabine was my best hope. When I led her out to the pavilion, I told her not to struggle, that I'd go easy on her if she'd help me and mine escape. Help put an end to this." He snuffled again. "All's she had do was pretend to fight, and I'd set her free after the show. Told her where to hide beneath the Grange aux Dimes. Told her to come back for us. Kill Gandler."

"And Theron?"

Kettle stopped and stared at me almost blankly, as if he had forgotten what we were talking about. Then, after a few seconds, he said, "Lord, but if you're not an impatient creature." He scratched his head and wiped at another smear of blood on his bandage. "I told Theron nothing. Never did trust the man myself. But then again, I'm not a dog person." Kettle laughed and then pulled himself together.

"Sabine must have given him a signal."

"Yes. But it's you I need, Feathers. You or someone like you. Someone to match Karl's strength. Gandler has Karl with him day and night."

"Kettle, I cannot."

"What? Not even with a belly full of that poor girl's blood? Not even with Joslyn's help?"

An icy chill ran down my spine. "How did she come to be here? She should not be here." It was all I could do to keep my voice at a whisper.

"Don't scowl at me. She was Sabine's doing. Sabine sought her out. Said Joslyn was the only preternatural being she knew she could count on to come to your aid, 'ceptin' herself. What is she, Feathers, a former lover?"

"Amedeo," I corrected him. "And no!" My denial came too forcefully.

Kettle trembled and tried to wriggle his deformed body back from the wagon a little.

"A former child," I whispered.

Kettle guffawed. "Well, we're all former children, aren't we? Regardless, with her help and Sabine's, and Lee and Theron, we can defeat Gandler."

I rattled the bars. "Then get me out of here."

"That, I cannot do." Kettle spread his hands before him. "Gandler has revoked my right to your key, and to mine own legs. Lee had to carry me here, left me under the wagon so I wouldn't be seen." His voice turned bitter. "And where was Sabine then? Where was Theron when Gandler was sawing off my legs? You are lucky, Feathers, to have so many care for you, and yet you would send Joslyn away."

My sigh was of sheer exasperation. "Where is Sabine now? I need to see her, to talk to her."

"Beneath the city. We are laying plans, Feathers. Joslyn is playing her part."

"And these plans, where I do I fit in them? When shall I break free of these damnable bars?" I kicked one angrily. Shook them with all my might so that the entire wagon trembled and threatened to roll.

Kettle's words rattled through his teeth as he said, "Shhh. Joslyn had seduced the old man. Every night she retires to his tent. Soon, the plan will play out. He will trust her enough to send Karl away, and she will kill him, drain him dry."

"Ridiculous!" I spat. "Gandler knows what she is. How could he not? He has been hunting her kind his entire life. And when he is sure, he will do to her what he did to Danette. What he did to you!" I gestured to Kettle's ruined legs. "She must leave this place. Leave it at once. You must promise me she will not go to his tent tonight." I crashed into the bars again, and despite myself, boomed, "Don't toy with me, Dwarf! She must not do this! Tell Sabine, too. Flee! Leave this accursed place. I will not have them do this for me."

"So selfish for an angel." Kettle's tone soured. "Do you think you are the only freak in this show who deserves his freedom? Do you think he won't torture my Giselle as easily as your Joslyn or your precious Sabine, whose teeth and claws grow back each night? Do you think Trudie or Seamus and Sinbad not worthy of living their lives? No, Sabine shall be my saving grace, even if you are too proud to let her be yours, Feathers. All woman she may be to you, Cruxim, but she has the heart of a lioness. I will not deny her this chance to pounce. She is waiting for it. She owes it to me. The lioness will have her kill."

Two nights later, Karl came for me. It was long after witching hour, and even the owls were stilled. Lee had long since curled up on his cloak to nap at the base of the wagon. I had heard nothing from Kettle, Sabine, or Joslyn. Had all been lost?

"Feathers, get up!" Karl towered over the wagon for a moment and then bent down to prod a javelin in through the bars.

I sniffed. "I'm nocturnal."

"I don't care what you are." He propped the javelin against the wagon. "Get up. I got a job for you." As Karl slid back the bronze bolt to unfasten the door of my cage, I reached out and snatched the javelin, drawing it in through the bars and then stabbing it out at Karl's unprotected belly.

He gave a bray of pain and then sprang open the door, and one hairy fist smashed me in the face. His aim was off, but he was quick, and the force of it drove me back against the bars. With the other hand, he wrenched the javelin back and flung it away onto the grass. His wrist, wide as a small cannon and as strong as steel, clutched mine, and he jerked me toward him. "Give me your other hand."

"Where's Kettle?"

"Shhh!" He squeezed my wrist and I felt the bones shift and begin to crack like half-dry kindling thrown on a fire. "Your hand, or I'll smash your pretty head so hard into these bars you'll break your otherworldly neck."

"Try it."

Karl's nostrils twitched and the ripple of a sneer tugged at his lip. "Your hand, Feathers," he said, squeezing again until I thought my wrist might snap.

Remembering Kettle's words, I gave him my other hand, watching as he tied them together with a length of thick rope.

"Now walk!" He jerked the rope, and I stumbled forward.

The grass was wet with dew, and a reluctant moon scythed low in the sky. Long shadows moved with us toward the far end of the row of covered wagons. Under a yew tree stood Gandler's tent of dark silk, candlelight silhouetting the figures inside.

Karl flung back the tent flap to reveal Joslyn standing over Gandler. Her dress was torn to the navel on one side, and one of Gandler's hands cupped her right breast. It was as perfect as I remembered, and I quickly turned away.

"He comes." Gandler's grin was skeletal. He looked different somehow; even more than usual, his face radiated evil.

The old man was dying, I realized. How many ghouls were waiting to tend on him in hell? He sat upon a bed made of hide stretched over a wooden frame.

"I told you." Joslyn gently pushed at his chest, easing him back down. "Soon, the Cruxim will be dead, and you and I will be immortal. What rulers of the underworld we will be. But you must have something to drink when you are newly made." The firelight made her features angular, wolfish. It suited her. She had never been more beautiful.

"And the Sphinx," Gandler wheezed. "I want her too. If I can't find her anchorstone before I die, I will nightly keep her pretty head on a pole and feed her bitch's body to the pigs in the marketplace."

"You will have her, too," Joslyn soothed. "The lioness.

119

I promise. Justice, strength, beauty and immortality all be yours this night, my Lord."

What act was this?

"You are certain that he is a Cruxim and that this will work? He was not listed in the book. Why should I believe a Vampire would know how to kill a Cruxim?" Gandler pointed one arthritic finger at the incunabulum, which sat on a wooden butcher's block to Joslyn's right, next to a rough wooden cot. A motion from the butcher's block drew my eye and a muffled squeal made it clear that the bound bundle that sat atop it was not a cheese or a package of goods but Kettle, trussed up like a Christmas ham.

"You are right. The Cruxim was not in the book. An oversight?"

I knew Joslyn's question was directed at me. I had given the book to her all those years ago, after all.

"You know how long I have searched for him," she soothed Gandler. "How long I have studied him. Trust me!" Joslyn turned to Kettle. "Now, now, this won't hurt a bit."

Gandler's clawed hand clenched her breast. "Not as much as I will hurt you if this fails," he warned Joslyn. "It will work perfectly, or it won't be Kettle's life I take first." Grabbing the rosy bud of her nipple, he twisted it cruelly.

Joslyn gasped, but covered it with a laugh.

What farce was this? She had not yet looked at me. And Kettle? Had she forsaken us both?

"It will work," she said. "He may be stronger than us, able to move about in daylight, his senses more keenly attuned. But now... we have learned his secrets. Mortal blood is poison to him. The very thing that sustains me means death to him."

"Joslyn!" I struggled to free myself from Karl's grasp. "Joslyn!" I yelled. "What have you done to me?"

Still she did not look at me. Her voice came strong and sour. "Karl, bind him."

With a great jolt, Karl swung me around onto the stretcher.

The air thumped out of me, and my wrists smarted. Blood flowed from my crucifixion wounds like stigmata, but I managed to croak out, "No!" and in a fit of rage, I pounded his brawny chest with both hands, all the while screaming.

From the look on the man's face, the paleness of his brow, I could tell my visage scared him, but he pushed me down on the contraption as if I were a child, tying my legs first. Then he stretched both arms out to the corners and fastened them with rope, double knotted and tight enough to score my flesh.

All the while, I gnashed my teeth, hissed, and writhed, resisting until he drew forth a handkerchief and made to gag me with it.

"Let him be, Karl. A gag is not necessary," Joslyn said.

"Let me hear his anguish," Gandler agreed. I could tell it excited him. Such was his tyranny that torture and public shame were his only excitements.

Still Joslyn did not look at me. She strode to the butcher's block and carefully took up something off it. Squinting into the light, she inspected what appeared to be a hollow glass tube. A syringe, I identified. "Soon this will be all be over, Ame." Her tone was gentle. "Do you remember, my angel, that night in the ruined castle?"

She turned to the side, the arm holding the implement obscured, and finally glanced over at me. Was it wistfulness or the sting of wounded pride that I detected in her profile?

"How could I forget the worst day of my life?" I spat.

Her beautiful face twisted for an instant. Then her expression calmed and her eyes became cold blue jewels in the steely helm of her face. "And what a long life you have lived," she said gaily. "But of course you remember. That night we both discovered that things were not as they seemed. Yet life still has not taught you that lesson properly: that men are easily deceived. That things are not always what they seem. It is a charming quality. Trust." She stared at me intently.

"Once, when I was a boy, I found a nest of starlings," I told her. "I warmed them daily with my own hands, but when the eggs hatched none but one survived. It was a cuckoo, I later learned. But I loved it as if I had laid the egg myself."

"A charming analogy." Her eyes flashed. "A reminder that beasts might betray as easily as humans, perhaps."

What did she mean by that? Had Sabine forsaken me too? Or had Joslyn promised Gandler Sabine's head on a pike? What treachery was this, or what game?

"Joslyn, I tire. Your quarrel is centuries old, and your enemy lies helpless here before you," Gandler snapped. "Give me immortality before infirmity overtakes me." He coughed. Joslyn plucked the handkerchief from Karl's hand and held it to his lips. Speckles of blood quickly colored it.

"Very well. Kettle, your arm." Joslyn moved to the butcher's block and bent low over the dwarf. Taking up a small knife in her left hand, she leaned across the dwarf's wriggling, grotesque body to slash the ties that bound his right arm. Then she leant further still, and I saw the brief gleam of glass.

Kettle made muffled protests through the gag, and the stumps of his missing legs squirmed as if to kick. It sickened me. Then he was still, his chest rising and falling as he stared at me imploringly. I strained against my bonds, but it was no use.

Gandler's hack became a gurgling laugh of approval. "She takes blood like she was born to it," he said, as if in conversation.

"She was," I answered coldly. "November the 12th, 1538, Joslyn was born to it. And she has taken it ever since. She has dabbled in blood and danced in it and traded in it, and you are a fool, old man, to give her yours.

A tyrant and a fool."

"I will give her your blood, too, Cruxim!" Gandler spat.

Joslyn smiled, but her eyes did not. "He remembers my birthday! How sweet of him."

"Inject him," Gandler cried. "And he will remember no more."

"Before we do this. You must tell us where you keep the keys. Your charges will starve to death should something happen, and Karl has served you admirably." She patted Gandler's hand.

"What need?" Gandler slumped back on the pillow, his veined, shaking hand seeking her breast again, but she shook him off.

"I will tell you after," he said.

"But, my Lord, you are an old man. To bestow immortal life is a long, tiring process, and one not without deprivations for one so frail. If something should happen to you."

I felt Karl's body stiffen. "Tell her, Gandler!"

"Yes, tell us. You would not let an old lady starve to death, my Lord," Joslyn insisted.

"He would not," Karl boomed, and a blob of his spittle landed on my face. "Have I not served you well, Master?"

Gandler's sneering laughter threw more blood into the handkerchief. "If I tell you now, Karl, you might kill me while I sleep, before I grow into my full strength. What idiot do you take me for? No, I'll tell you after."

"Very well, then," Joslyn cooed. She moved to Gandler's bed and stroked his face, pushing it to face the silken wall, revealing his wrinkled throat. "I shall take you now. Take you first, my Lord."

"Silence!" Gandler hissed, and his arm clutched hers. "While he is still alive? The Cruxim who might destroy me and you both? You will do no such thing. I will see him die first. Only then is my immortality assured."

Joslyn bent her head to inspect the syringe again.

"Master, these things are never assured. You are an old man, and once drained you will require my blood and then the blood of another to feed upon. A newborn Vampire should ideally drink little at first. Kettle will be just a snack, his blood enough to tide you over until I can bring you the wolfman."

On the butcher's block, Kettle squirmed again and mumbled through his gag.

"Bring him Trudie," Karl suggested. "She'd make a big meal. Or the lioness."

"What have you done with her?" I screamed. "I will kill you both for this."

"When we are stronger, we will dispose of the lioness together," Joslyn told Gandler.

"Good. She has a debt to pay—a blood debt. Now, do it!" Gandler urged. "Enough of this infernal talk. Kill him, or I shall do it myself." He made to snatch the syringe, but Joslyn held it away.

Her lips pursed. Then she reached out with her other hand to stroke Gandler's balding pate. "Precautions, my Lord. Remember I have done this before. You have not. It is natural to be afraid, to be cautious. Tell us where the keys are, just in case."

Gandler's eyes burned. "Nothing will happen to me, you bitch, or I shall haunt you to the gates of hell." He pointed a quivering finger at me, his face near apoplectic with age and anticipation. "Now inject him. I will tell Karl afterward, to thank him for his service."

Joslyn approached my bed, leaning over me so close that I could smell her: she smelled as she always had, of rosemary and regret, and some tincture I could not define. Betrayal? Guilt? Desire! Even after all these centuries. Some part of it smelled just as my hope had tasted, high in the tower of Sezanne.

I struggled, not to escape her, but in my longing for her.

Obligation coursed through me. Need and desire. *Rise up and take her! Kill her! Own her*, my heartbeat thrummed. *You must.* But Karl had tied my arms tautly up near my head and even with every muscle tensed, my frantically jerking neck could not reach hers.

"Death is a dream," she whispered, bending low over my arm. "And life is a curse. Nothing is ever as it seems." She stroked the juncture of my inner elbow, her fingertips gentling out the vein. The cool touch drew my hot blood like a magnet. Then she slid the needle into me and quickly pushed the plunger all the way in. I felt the adrenalin course through me, bucking my body with a sudden sweet rapture, and then ... nothing.

How sweet oblivion is after torment. Cool and still, it filled and hollowed me at the same time. And when its rapturous blackness gave way to a dull, weak light above, I heard the voices. At first, I thought it a host of Seraphim, singing me to my Maker. The unnatural surging in my veins, the ecstasy that, since my confinement in Sezanne tower, I had felt only at the taste of Danette's blood began to subside. Then the words themselves seemed to grow wings like bumblebees and buzz in the gauze of air around me, gradually becoming clearer.

"Untie him."

"Mademoiselle?"

"Untie him! He is dead. What can a dead man do to you, Karl?"

A lot, I thought. *A dead man is the most dangerous kind.*

I tried to swivel my eyes to see who spoke but could not. My eyelids were heavy, my vision opaque. Over the shallow cadence of my own pulse, I could hear Karl bustling about my body. Rope being untied. Sensation began to trickle back to my fingers like a runnel of water back into the sea.

"If Gandler should die, I will kill you myself."

Karl's thick threat.

Then a laugh. Hers. Sweet as a brook's song. "I did not know you cared so much for Gandler. He won't die, not unless I let him." She moved to my side. "I have drained him of blood. He is just weak, that is all. It is part of the process of becoming a Vampire."

"You shouldn't have done this! You should have made him tell you where he was keeping them." I made out Kettle's voice.

"How did you get the gag off, little man?" Karl.

"Leave him," commanded Joslyn. "He is harmless. Soon, he will be Gandler's first meal anyway. What he overhears is irrelevant." She turned to Kettle. "Anyway, you heard him. What could I do? He refused to reveal it until after the Cruxim was dead."

"Stupid," Kettle growled. "Why would he tell you now? Once he is immortal, he will rule over us forever. What need does he have to tell? He will never let them go."

"He is weak. Look at him. His breath comes so slightly. Only Vampire blood will make him immortal now. If I do not let him drink from me, he will die within hours, but first he will tell us what we need to know."

"He better. Then a savage hell awaits him."

"No!" Karl's voice. "He moved them all, Kettle. All of his 'insurances,' as he calls them. If he dies, so do they." I heard Karl's heavy footsteps moving in the direction of Joslyn's voice. "If you let him die, you fanged bitch, I will force this into your heart."

How I wished I could see, or move my limbs, but every part of my body was as cold and unyielding as stone. Was this the nightmare Sabine lived daily, ensconced in stone, hearing, feeling but with no way of communicating? Even my groan seemed far away. If only I could find a way to move!

But what would I do, even if I could? Save the woman

who had just betrayed me? Kill the monstrosity that lay wretched on the bed? Or wrestle the man with the strength of ten men who had made Gandler's freakshow possible?

A sudden yowling, snarling creature burst into the tent, startling me into the strange sensation of falling.

Sabine!

Blood warmed me and rushed to my extremities, but my motions were still stiff and groggy. I lurched to my feet, crashed against the wooden table, stumbled to my knees, and cried out, "Sabine!"

A blur of tawny fur and exposed teeth rushed past me. In the corner, I saw a smaller, darker figure grappling with Karl's bulk. Gandler's Herculean bodyguard had Theron by the neck, crushing the life out of him. One enormous, tree-trunk leg was busy trying to kick off Sabine, whose teeth gripped his ankle. She evaded him and pounced at Karl's giant chest, a whirl of claws and lashing tail.

"Ame!"

Spinning clumsily around, I confronted Joslyn, my throat dry with bloodlust.

"No!" she called, throwing her hands up as I lurched towards her. "It is not what you think. I tried to warn you of that."

"You betrayed me. Tried to kill me!" My speech was slurred, but another surge of strength egged me on. I half-leaped, half-swooped down on her, my hands clawing at her throat. "To make him a Vampire? A narcissist. A torturer. He would be an overlord. Worse than Beltran." I wrenched her to me and pushed her head aside, exposing the curved lines of her neck, ready to bury myself in her veins. To end this.

"Feathers, stop!" A piercing pain shot through my calf. "Stop this!" And then another.

Glancing down, I saw Kettle plunging the syringe into my leg. "Stop this madness. Karl is your enemy, not Joslyn."

"All Vampires are my enemy, Dwarf. Especially those

who have betrayed me. Those who tried to kill me."

"By God's balls! She did not try to kill you, Feathers. She tried to free you."

"Free me? From life? What a fine euphemism. And Gandler?" I threw out a hand towards where he lay feebly on his cot. "You would have him immortal?"

"I would have him in his grave, you fool! And so would she. But look at him." Kettle's stubby finger pointed to where Karl stood bellowing like a newly castrated bull in the corner. He had thrown Sabine off once more. Despite the blood that spurted from his forehead, Karl launched himself onto Theron with a shriek, in his rage upending a chest containing instruments. The clatter filled my ears like the paean of some almighty battle.

"What hope would we have of defeating Gandler and Karl without you? Even with Joslyn, Sabine is injured, and Theron is no wolf; he is just a man. And then there is me, Cruxim. A small man with big hopes. You think we could defeat Karl without you?"

I saw then how Sabine favored her left forepaw and the black smear of blood from a deep gash on her shoulder.

"We needed your strength. Needed you out of that cage."

"Gandler is old," Joslyn rasped.

I eased my hold on her throat. In the corner, Sabine snarled at Karl, who had paused, listening. His eyes were fixed on Joslyn. Theron lay crumpled and lifeless at his feet.

"And old men are afraid of their mortality," Joslyn continued. "All these years he has hated us, but still he would rather join us than die like a man. It was my opportunity to kill him."

"What did you promise him, Joslyn!" My hands moved to her throat again, and fear widened those beautiful eyes. "Only this." She swept a hand over her body. "And Sabine's death, and yours. But that was a lie. The blood was mine, Ame. Mine! Mixed with a heavy dose of laudanum to make you appear dead. I drew it out while I spoke to you, when I asked you if you remembered that night near the Convent of Angels, while I warned you that sometimes things are not as they seem."

I remembered the sharp look of pain that had crossed her face. I had thought it was at my words, those cruel but true words, but in truth, it had been the bite of the needle in her vein.

"Then, once he told us where he kept his prisoners," she continued, "I would drain Gandler of his blood, and you would rouse and defeat Karl and Gandler both."

"You would deceive and defeat me!" yelled Karl. "Why must you all hate me so? I despise the man. I would choke him myself if only I knew where my mother was." Karl raised his hands in a show of surrender. "Let me be, and I will force it out of him myself."

Sabine snarled but did not leap again. Her green eyes bore into him, watching for any movement.

"What now, Kettle?" I called, pushing Joslyn away from me. I felt stupid, angry. Dissatisfied. Her blood still hummed in me, and my body craved it more than the laudanum. "Why did you not tell me?" I screamed at all of them.

"Gandler had to believe your death." It was Sabine who answered. "And you had to believe it."

"Had you known it was laudanum, that it was my blood," said Joslyn, "you might have—"

"What?" I cut her off. "Attacked you? Killed him? Let me strangle him now. Would you give up your children, Kettle, to spare the world a Vampire like Gandler?"

"No!" Karl bellowed from the corner. He charged forward again, his right leg planting a kick in Sabine's left ribs as he rushed towards Gandler's bed. Sabine whimpered, and then a growl burst from her. A flap of her wings propelled her after him, but I could see she was hurt. Instead, Joslyn sprang for Karl, teeth bared, but he pushed past her to me.

"I will kill Gandler myself if you can force him to reveal where she is."

"She must turn him," Kettle agreed. "And then, when we know where he has imprisoned them, Amedeo must kill him."

The thought of Gandler's death tempted me.

"Joslyn…" The voice came thinner than the pale horizon that separates night from day. "Joslyn, I am so thirsty. Come to me. I need you."

"No. Finish this," I commanded. "Finish what you began. Drink from him. Drain him. Leave him a shell, a dead mortal. We cannot take the risk of him becoming immortal."

"Yes, it is too dangerous!" Sabine's breathy voice was laced with pain. "Kill him now."

"And let my children die!" Kettle screeched.

A monstrous roar filled the air as Karl pummeled the makeshift table with one enormous fist. With the other, he snatched up Joslyn by the hair and pushed her down on top of Gandler's bony body. "Drink!" he commanded Gandler. "Drink from her."

"No!" I swooped into the air, kicking at the gigantor's flat-nosed face, but Karl swatted me away one-handed. As Sabine flapped up to assist me, she copped the full force of Karl's fist in the chest. With a hiss of breath, she crumpled back to the ground. "Ame," she cried. "Stop him!"

From below came a slow, steady mewling, a slurping like an infant at the breast. A stream of sticky blood pooled at the corner of Gandler's mouth.

"Sweet," he murmured, and I saw the veins in his hands throb as he held Joslyn's throat to his lips.

"Release her!" Sabine winced and leaped at Karl again, but her claws found no purchase and a blow to the jaw felled her with a groan. Still I flapped and punched and pushed at the mountainous man before me.

"It is too much!" Joslyn panicked, struggling against

Karl's one-handed grasp. "He wants too much of me. He drinks too much. Make him stop," she wailed. "Oh, Ame, make him stop."

"Tell me where my mother is, Master, if you want more," Karl commanded Gandler. "Or I wrench her from you!"

But still the puckered lips kept on, draining the color from Joslyn's face and body.

Karl wrenched Joslyn backward, his hand still knotted in her hair, and Gandler gasped as his lips sucked air.

"More!" Gandler snatched at her. "More!" Springing forward, he latched his newly minted fangs onto Joslyn's bare breast and the awful slurping began again.

Again, Karl wrenched her away.

Joslyn was sobbing now, moaning.

"Where do you keep my mother, old man?" Karl shrieked.

"Not old man, no." Gandler's black eyes gleamed as he flexed his hands. "Not even man." He cackled. The age spots, wrinkles, and prominent veins were replaced with skin taut with the healthy glow of blood. Hair grew thick and black from his crown, and muscles rippled in his chest. "More!" He sprang forward again. Once more, Karl stopped him.

"No more! Not more unless you tell me."

"Out of town, on the Ruelle aux Vignes." Gandler licked his scarlet-stained lips. "There is a tannery. There, in the basement."

"You would not lie to me, old man. My mother is alive?"

"And Giselle? Kellane?" Kettle, on the floor, wriggled closer.

"Yes. They are. They are yours. The key is there." He pointed to a small wooden chest that sat near the incunabulum. "Release them. Just give me this!" Gandler reached for Joslyn again. The strength of his fingers left instant dark bruises on her flesh.

"No!" Joslyn screamed, struggling from the bed. "Enough!" Blood streamed down her breast to stain her dress.

"I will say what is enough!" Encouraged by the Vampire blood that coursed through his veins, Gandler tugged her closer. Then his eyes sparkled as they fixed on Karl's meaty paw. Tossing Joslyn aside, Gandler grabbed Karl's hand, sank his fangs into the wrist with an audible crunch, and began to suck.

With a scream of terror, Karl threw up his hands, trying vainly to dislodge the beast clamped onto his wrist.

"Ame! It is time." Joslyn stumbled away from them both, toward the butcher's block, and clutched it to steady herself. "Kill him. Do it now."

"Get him off!" Karl screamed, flinging his arm around wildly. "Off!" In his panic, he knocked over one of the candles. Gandler leaped for Karl's throat, and the enormous man stumbled backwards, his weight coming down on Sabine and pulling the fabric of the tent down around him. The tent collapsed in on itself, and with a whoosh, the silk ignited.

Flapping desperately, I shot up into the air, hauling some silk after me.

"Sabine! Joslyn!" Like a falcon I plunged into the mess of writhing bodies, smoke, and black silk, searching for Sabine's yellow hair or twitching tail, or for Joslyn's pale form, screaming their names incessantly.

"Ame!" Joslyn emerged first. She clutched the incunabulum and the trinket box, and blood and ash stained her cheeks as she stared heavenward. "Behind you." Her whisper was almost ghostly.

"Where is Sabine?" I screamed.

"Behind you!" She pointed.

"Where is Sabine!" My head swiveled in the direction of her trembling finger. "What have you done to—" My words were deafened by the screech of a thousand descending bats.

"Did you think I would let you go, you silly, silly pretty

little thing? Did you think I hadn't heard of Gandler's Circus of Curiosities and his new acts?"

I recognized Beltran's voice as the first of the bats struck my face with its wings, slicing my cheek. Immediately, the creature became Beltran. He grabbed Joslyn's arm. Fangs bared, he turned to me and screamed, "Did you think I would let you have her?"

I ignored him. "Sabine!" I cried, plummeting back into the inferno, where I could make out a golden shape being consumed by flame. My wings smoldered and the feathers curled in the heat, but I flew on to her, and with all my strength I lifted her to my chest. Smoke choked me, and her unconscious weight meant I could barely lift her more than six feet above the burning tent. The yew tree, too, was aflame, sending plumes of smoke up to hide the squalling bats that wheeled overhead. I fluttered above the flames until the smoke cleared, and then I made to land on the grass.

"No!" A monster sprang from the fire. A newly born Vampire with incredible strength. "The Sphinx is mine!" Gandler pitched himself at me, knocking me to my knees.

"She promised." He pointed at Joslyn.

Beltran still clutched Joslyn two handed, and his eyes burned with hatred for me and with lust for her.

"She lied!" I bellowed. With a roar, I dropped Sabine on the grass and sprang at Gandler, pinning him backward. When my teeth found the hollow near his collarbone, I bit down with all my force. His blood rushed up to greet me. But his strength was amazing, as if the strength of Karl had flowed into him. He launched me back with a squeal, and a score or more of his Vampire cronies descended on me. The bats' claws struck my face, split my lips, and tore at my eyes. Ever more spilt from the sky like a black rain until they surrounded me, their screeches drowning out Joslyn's sobs.

I shot upwards, the only route afforded me, but still they clung to my clothes and wings, biting, tearing at my feathers until, lifted airborne with me, they morphed into Vampires to try to weigh me back down. I sank my teeth into one, drinking my fill in seconds, and then another. When their blood coursed through me, I found the strength to shake and kick the others off.

Beltran's twisted laugh spewed out overhead as I spiraled up through the flock of bats.

"He does not want you, my love," Beltran taunted Joslyn. "I have come all this way for you, and look at him—he would prefer a beast. A freak."

Joslyn just stared at him passively, still clutching the book.

Beltran reddened her cheek with a slap, then took her face in his hands. "Yet still you love him?" The word was a vile thing in his mouth. "How many centuries have you loved him? Oh, it stings, Joslyn. It stings so: to love and not be loved." His lips twisted into a smile, which he pressed down hard on her mouth.

Joslyn silently turned her head away.

It was all I could do not to fly down to her again, outnumbered as I was, and destroy Beltran forever.

Weeping then, she pulled away, and Beltran let her go. "He does not want you," he taunted. Then, with a shove, "And nor do I. I have had you. I had you first, remember." He turned to the pack of grinning Vampires and commanded, "Take the cat instead!"

"She's mine." Gandler flew at Beltran and pushed him backward. "She has a blood debt to pay."

Beltran looked Gandler up and down, taking in his bulging muscles, the neck thick as an ox's, the arms like steel. "You made this, Joslyn?" Beltran sounded surprised as he gestured to the newborn Vampire. "Impressive." Turning back to his henchman, he said, "Bring him too. I can use a man of his power."

"Noooo!" I screamed, hurtling down, rushing at the Vampires who were manhandling Sabine's body into what was left of the silk tent. But there were too many. One caught my right wing and I felt the tendons tear and cried out in pain.

"Sabine!" My voice was hoarse with failure as I rose above them again, more weakly this time. Resigned to my fate, I let both wings drop and felt my body begin to descend, but a single small bat shot up from below. It clung to my chest, close to my heart. "No," it said in Joslyn's voice. "Fly. Fly now! It is nearly dawn."

She was right. The sun stirred above the horizon. All around, the bats began to scatter. Taking up the silk in their claws and mouths, they wheeled as one to carry Sabine's shrouded body south.

Exhausted, I collapsed to the ground, where the bodies of Kettle, Karl, and Theron still burned. It was only when the sun's disk was nearly fully risen above the horizon that I noticed Joslyn, a Vampire again now, still crushed against my chest.

"Joslyn, the sun," I said, shielding her. Blood gathered at her throat like lace, and my longing almost overwhelmed me.

"It is true," she said, still weeping. "What he said is true. You do not want me. You love Sabine. Let me die here, Ame." She struggled to free herself from my embrace. "Just let me burn."

I pushed her hair back from her tear-stained cheeks.

"Or else take me. Take what is left of me so that you might have the strength to go after her." She bowed her head.

"No." I crushed her cold body back to my chest and, thrusting the trinket box and incunabulum back into her arms, rose up with her, my damaged wings and wrists aching like my heart, headed for the Grange aux Dîmes.

TWELVE

All day, I paced while Joslyn slept. The tunnels concealed us from the prying eyes of man, and we crept deep into the darkness, both of us burrowing into our own private pain. When she slept, Joslyn looked so vulnerable that even sharing a room with her was an effort, so sometime mid-afternoon I left our passage beneath the tithe barn and made my way to the remains of the tent.

Cinders still stirred in the grass, but Lee had moved the bodies of Karl, Theron, and his father back inside the wagons.

I approached Lee cautiously.

"He was a good man," I said, placing one hand on Lee's shoulder.

He immediately shrugged me off. "He was a man, at least. What are you?" He rushed at me, shoved me. "You caused this. I saw what she did to him. He was bound, as if a legless man was at risk to escape. And Gandler, where is he? Now Giselle and my brother must rot somewhere while my father and this monster"—he gestured to Karl's body on the wagon—"are in their graves? You caused this. Until you came, we were men at least, freaks or no, but now?

"What are you, Feathers? I used to think angels would do God's bidding, but this"—he wiped his ash-smeared face with the back of his hand—"this is Satan's duty. Everything is burned to ashes." He gestured to the remains of the tent. "And Giselle and Kellane will surely starve to death."

"It is not what you think," I told him. "I know where your sister and Kellane are. I have the key."

He nodded mutely, and I saw what I identified as hope cross his face. "You will free them?"

"I have freed you all." But my heart added, *At what dear price?*

It was late afternoon before I made it to the Ruelle aux Vignes. The pungent odor of decaying flesh, urine, and lime assaulted my nostrils before I had even drawn close to the tannery. Slowly, Danette's blood, Joslyn's, and the blood of the Vampires I had dispatched was reinvigorating me. My Cruxim senses were returning. I could feel the blood in my veins, could almost hear it swelling my heart.

Had they died here, no one would have suspected a thing. I thought of Kettle, his determination to seek freedom for his children, and felt I had failed him as surely as I failed Sabine. At least she had been able to run or to fly. I had barely considered Kettle. In truth, I had let him burn.

The tannery seemed deserted. I pushed open the door and entered the vile-smelling place. The walls and floor were lined with filth, and the abrasive lime stung my skin. The air on the stairs that led to the basement reeked of death, but I did not find death below in the dungeon.

"Who goes there?" called a voice watery with age. "Karl?"

"None you know, old woman, but I am not your jailer, nor your son."

"Executioner then?" a boy's voice said. "Has he finally

decided to end our torment?"

"No, but I have. I have come to release you." I moved out of the darkness and into the bars of thin light thrown by the basement's only window.

A gasp came from the cage, and a child, who was obviously Giselle, rushed to the bars. "Look at his skin, at his eyes. It is one of them," she wailed. "Stay away from us!" She clutched Kellane's leg. "It was not me. I did not do it to her. He made me help him. He forced me!"

Kellane stepped in front of them both, his scarred face cynical.

"Come, child." The old woman lifted Giselle onto her lap.

"How do we know you mean us no harm?" Kellane asked.

"Your father told me everything. May your mother, Kira's, ghost pursue me if lie. I mean to free you only."

Still the girl sobbed. "I ... I did nothing," she said again, shaking her head.

I realized Giselle must have meant Danette. Kettle had mentioned that Gandler used the child as an assistant to his vile acts.

I strode to the door, slid the key into the lock, and turned it, which set the girl wailing again, sure her reckoning was coming. Pushing open the squeaky door, I said simply, "There. Use your freedom well. Life is short."

"Mine more than theirs," the old woman's croak followed me. "Tell me, creature, what have you done with my son, Karl?"

"He is dead," I told her, feeling for her but nothing for him. "Gandler killed him." I supposed it was true, in a way.

"And my father?" Kellane stepped after me as I made my exit.

"Dead also. I am sorry."

Giselle sobbed out, "I am sorry. I never meant to hurt her."

Crouching, I wiped her face with one hand. "She knew.

Go with your brothers. Lee also still lives."

"And where should I go?" The old woman hobbled past me. "My life is spent, and my son is dead. How should I go on?"

"In peace, mother." I put my hand on her arm. "Go in peace."

When I returned to the caverns beneath the Grange aux Dîmes, it was already evening, and they were vacant. I searched them all to no avail until I remembered to trust the lure of her blood, the senses I had neglected for so long. The piquant scent of Vampire blood on the breeze soon led me to the Tower Cesar, where I found Joslyn watching the moonrise, its curved horns rising like a warning.

"You should have left me there," she said, pulling the ruined white dress around her shoulders. "I wanted you to leave me."

I sighed and sank onto the sandstone of the window nearest her. "You used to be so full of joy."

"Yes, I was alive then. Now I am full of death. So many little deaths."

"And yet you walk and talk and eat ... and love." I inspected an ant, winding over the sandstone.

"Yes, I love," she said sharply. "Someone who cannot love me. Someone whose heart is a stone sitting in a vault somewhere. Someone who has forsaken me."

I could not see her face, but I could smell the bloody tears that pricked her eyes.

"God has forsaken you, Joslyn. I never have." I stood again, weary of this talk. After two centuries. Could love endure so much death, so many betrayals, so much blood and pain? And yet I loved her still.

A breeze lifted a curl from her shoulder and tugged it away from her neck. I watched it for a moment, focused on the bite marks Gandler had left on her. Bloodlust burned in me like passion. I turned away to watch the moonlight silver the poplars, which pointed to the deviled moon. "I have always loved you," I said.

She spun, the sooty white silk wrapping her, and rushed to me, but I put up my hands and moved away until my back hugged the stone.

"Then come with me," she urged, pressing herself to me anyway. "Ame, come with me. There are places we can be together, places deep in the Hindu Kush where you think your blood might freeze. Places where the moon sits on a mountaintop and is reflected threefold in a lake that stretches out of sight. Places where Beltran will never find us. Please." Her words had the poignancy of tears, but it was her blood that quickened me. My need for her rose up like a terrible inferno until my lips were just a whisper away from her neck. Then an unassailable anger replaced my desire. What monster had I become?

Inching backward, I let myself fall from the window ledge and then hovered there, outside. The pain that gripped my wings felt right, like penance.

Joslyn took a step back, her lips quivering.

"Please." My wings began to fail, so I stood on the window ledge. "I cannot bear for you to touch me. You must keep your distance."

Her face crumpled.

"Joslyn, you do not know what hell this is to long to embrace you and yet long to kill you. Just being here with you is a torture. Your blood..."

She put her face in her hands and wept. "I know longing. I cannot bear this longing anymore, Ame, and you cannot bear to even look at me." Throwing her head up, she commanded, "Do it. Do what you so desire to do. I can long for you no more. Let me die in your arms with your mouth at my throat. I beg you."

Joslyn's color was high, her eyes like sapphires. Her

loveliness and wildness and brash courage were undeniable, and burning inside me was a flame that could consume her.

"I cannot!" I thundered. "Do not ask this of me, Joslyn. I cannot do this."

But she was a woman, after all, and she knew how to use desire to her advantage. Stepping closer again, she begged, "You will have your Sabine, your purpose, your freedom. Would you leave me with nothing? All hope dashed, love conquered, nothing but this living death. The deaths of innocents to wither me for eternity. You would fill your life with love and hope and faith, and leave mine empty as a bone." She pressed forward again, embraced me closely so her face was pressed to my chest.

It was all I could do to grind the words out. "I gave you faith, Joslyn; you did not want it. I gave you love, but my love was not enough for you. Now what hope can I give you? You were innocent when he made you this, this ..." I pointed at her. "This creature." I looked away. "My only hope is that your innocence then might save you from hellfire, just as it might have saved her."

"Her?"

"The girl, Danette, whom Beltran made. I... I..."

"You killed her." Her eyes flashed. "You fed on her, and yet you would deny me my death. Why?" Her face was flushed and her blood showed as warm and thick as burgundy in her veins.

I held up my hands and then moved one to my temple. My head ached. "Joslyn, do not ask me to do this. I cannot do this."

"You promised me. You promised Beltran you would kill us both," she screamed. "I cannot do this. I cannot live on knowing that you would choose her over me, that you will never be mine. So make me yours in death." Sobs broke her words, and I could stand her tears no longer.

I remembered the euphoria I had felt on the stretcher

with a syringe full of her blood inside me, and I flew to her and seized her with more strength than I thought left in me.

"Amede—" she began, but I pressed my lips to hers until she swallowed my name deep into herself and found my tongue.

When her kiss turned sweet with blood and relief, I stroked her temple, feeling the pulse there weakening. I nuzzled the hollow behind her ear, ran my lips down the smooth plane of her neck to her unblemished shoulder, and drew her blood up to the skin's surface with my kiss.

"Yes," she whimpered as my fangs found her vein. "Please, Ame."

Her blood met me in rich streams and her heartbeat was a wild pounding in my head, like a drum in the night. But each beat came with a chorus of guilt. Danette's face flashed into my mind—that serene, devout young face—and I wrenched my lips away.

"I cannot." I leaped away from her.

"Fly then!" she screamed. "Fly away, just like before. Leave me in this darkness. Let me seek out the sunshine alone."

And, her blood having restored some strength to my wings, I did.

I could not bear to watch that sunrise. Sabine was gone, I knew not where, and now I had lost Joslyn too. An unquenchable sorrow and a hatred for Beltran and Gandler and all their kind gripped me, and although the day was bright, I felt darkened by it. Joslyn's exquisite blood still nourished me, and I considered where Beltran might have taken Sabine and what they might do to her. I longed to wreak immediate vengeance upon them, but the thought came to me that perhaps I should seek out Sabine's anchorstone. At least then I could guard it and move it somewhere safe to ensure her immortal soul would endure. But where to start? Had she told me the truth about the Hotel du Sully? I had to know for sure.

I crept deeper into the passageways beneath the Grange aux Dîmes, threading my way through them and heading north until I found a chamber I considered must be close to the ramparts. Stone steps rose up and I followed them out into the blinking-bright sunshine. The ramparts towered up before me. I hurried through the gates and immediately as I was out of sight of the ramparts, circled upward, high into the sky until the air was so thin it burned my lungs. From below, I might have resembled a large eagle, soaring through the heavens. Each flap of my damaged wings sent a spike of pain through me, but I ignored them all and pushed on toward Paris.

When I arrived, I made my way to Rue Saint-Antoine, in Marais. The hotel was fashionably Baroque with two stone Sphinxes guarding the entrance to the courtyard. I approached them cautiously, as if I were nothing but a passerby. They faced each other, their dead eyes blank. I saw little of Sabine in the mien of either of them but for the slight look of torment in their rigid faces. After approaching the one on the left, I ran my hand over its flanks and up to its face and hair. No one seemed to be around and the cobbled streets were quiet.

I leaned in and placed my lips upon the cold mouth of the first Sphinx. Nothing. Turning to its twin, I did the same, and this time my lips met her mouth, her cheek and her brow, but there was nothing but the feel of granite and the sniggering laugh of a small boy. Looking up, I caught a glimpse of the child in the upstairs window and I leaped back, one hand to my lips. For a moment, I stared once more into the faces of the two lifeless Sphinxes, wondering who they were, or what they were. Were women like Sabine locked within their stony frames, awaiting release?

Or were they nothing but adornments, not immortal but merely immobile, reminders of the guardians who bore their likeness? Deciding on the latter, I stepped back again and strode off in the direction I had approached. Disappointment churned in me, but what had I expected? Sabine had told me her anchorstone was not at the Hotel du Sully—was not even in Paris—and, indeed, there had been nothing there for me but humiliation. Yet still I wondered. Cryptic as I knew Sabine was, I questioned whether she had secretively meant to alert me to some other statue nearby, perhaps drawing a comparison. For hours, I wandered the streets of Paris, revisiting the many Sphinxes that embellished the city and at which I had searched for her on my liberation from the tower. On pained wings, I flew to the Place du Châtelet, but although the Sphinxes of the Fontaine du Palmier felt warmer to my touch, none were awakened to me. At the Hotel de Ville, a watchful female Sphinx who bore Sabine's beauty and regal bearing was unmoved by my kiss. I searched for Sabine's image at the Chateaux du Marais, but found her there neither. Nor did the sculptures of Château de Bagatelle, the Jardin des Tuileries, or the Musée du Louvre pay any mind to my Pygmalion hopes. When night fell, numb with grief and effort, I settled myself on the roof of the Louvre and wept.

Her velvety paw on my face was warm, warmer than her breath, which tickled my ear as she whispered to me, "Ame. Ame, you must listen. Do not wake, but hear this."

I stirred and must have tried to sit, but even in my dream, the gentle strength of her paw held me down and felt as real as if she were there herself. I felt her lips brush my ear and then my neck, and the feeling soothed my semi-lucid mind.

Sabine, I have tried to find you, I heard the dreaming voice in my head tell her, panicked. *Where are you? Where is your stone?*

Something told me my fear was that death had found her and that his black wings had carried her here, through the night, to my dreaming form.

"Hush," she said, a word as tender as any I had ever heard from her, and I felt her body fold down next to me, warm and animate, and as real as if we were curled up together. I tried to reach out to stroke her hair, but it was nothing but air.

Are you dead? My voice sounded small and strangled and far off, and already I was dreading her answer.

"No," she laughed but not without pain. "I live, Ame. I live for you."

Where? The panic returned. *Where are you, Sabine? God help me! I will tear them to pieces until I find you.*

"No!" Her tone was harsh. "There has been enough cruelty. So much cruelty as to make even a feline weep."

It struck me as strange to hear her refer to herself so. She had always considered herself wholly woman. But I had no doubt that beastly actions had driven her to me. I felt her lips on my wrist, and her warm tongue lapped at the trickle of blood that slithered from my crucified palms.

Again, I tried to sit, to stir and possibly even to wake to her, so tangible was the touch of her fur and the sensation of her lips, but again she stopped me.

"Come for me, but then let us leave this place. They have taken me to an island, a walled city overlooking some kind of strait. In a tower they confine me by day. I fight, of course, but they are strong, Ame. An army of undead."

Where is this place, Sabine?

"I know not, only that it is an island, several hours south-east yet still in France, and well defended." She fell silent.

Sabine? My heart cried out to her, worried she had vanished. *Have they hurt you?*

Mewling kisses peppered my face in answer and I lay

back, lost in the sensation and in the deep currents of loss and pain and hope that flowed through us both.

I cannot bear for them to hurt you. Tell me where your stone is, that I might keep it safe.

"Ame, I cannot. A Sphinx may reveal it only in riddles."

She was ever an enigma. *Then riddle me! Let me know!*

She paused, and even in my semi-lucid state, I knew she feared it would be of no use. Did I know her so little, after all this time?

"Where womb and navel meet as one, and python's coils foretell the sun, there shall you find the stone you seek, of marble smooth and white and sleek. Make a pledge to know thyself before mischief is nigh, and you shall know the ancient place at which my stone doth lie."

Go on, I heard myself urge.

She laughed. "There is no more, Ame."

But that makes no sense. I tried to commit it to memory but my mind was a fog.

She said nothing, just smiled sadly. "I cannot tell you more."

Sabine, you must! I cannot bear what they might do to you before I find you.

She said again in that mellifluous voice she used only for me, "Hush, my darling. Then forget the stone. What use is stone when the flesh desires? Come for me here. Find this island and come for me, and we shall flee accursed France forever, but do not fear for me, for I have two things they do not."

What do you have? My head was a mess of riddles and dreams.

"I have you. And I have faith."

I awoke with a start to find myself alone, my head against cold stone made warm with sleep's tears.

I sat up and rubbed my eyes, trying to discern the dream from reality. Had Sabine been real or a phantasm come to taunt me? I tried to call the riddle to my mind, but it was patchy and fragmented, fading into my subconscious. "Sabine!" I cried aloud. "Sabine, tell me more!" But she could not.

I paced the rooftop, pondering where the island she mentioned might be and trying to remember the riddle. Even if I could locate the island, my wings were so tender I doubted I could make it any further south than Provins. Just getting to Paris had been an effort.

Why? I cursed to myself, and my torn wings flapped in agitation. *Why do I know so little about everything? About Sphinxes and their riddles? About myself?* Then, as my despairing mind grappled to recall and decode Sabine's riddle, it settled on Gandler's face, hooded as he held up a book to the bars in the tower of Sezanne, mocking me with the image of a Sphinx.

The incunabulum! I had never read the entry. On finding the book centuries ago, I had not contemplated ever meeting a Sphinx. I had only flipped through, searching for my kind. When all trace of my species was absent, I had been disappointed at first, and then relieved, and then, I had given it to Joslyn. Perhaps the book mentioned something about a Sphinx's riddle, or how to find an anchorstone! Wincing at the pain I knew it would cause my wings, I swooped off the rooftop and headed back toward Provins.

Mid-morning, a gentle shaking woke me to the song of swallows in the chamber above. "Ame, awake."

"Sabine!" In my half-asleep state, I expected it to be another dream. But then I noticed the dark rough-hewn passage I was in and recognized the blue eyes. "Joslyn?" I rubbed my aching wings. I had not expected to see her again, perhaps ever. I had imagined she had been true to her word.

"Arise." Crouching down, she touched me again, and I

wondered if I were still dreaming.

"Joslyn, I told you: I cannot."

With a sad smile, she gazed down at her hands. Her eyes were red-rimmed, the lower lids heavy with the weight of tears. "I know. Be at peace. I have an idea where they may have taken Sabine."

"Sabine?"

"You love her," she whispered, as I righted myself and ran a hand through my hair. "And I love you," she continued. "I would not wish for you the loneliness I endure. All night once you left me last, I raged and wept, and before the sun rose I thought I would sit out in it, see the sun kiss the treetops one last time before I left you. But I could not." She stood and faced the wall of the tunnel. It was dark and cool, a cavern of limestone.

It reminded me suddenly of a grave, filled with her bereavement.

"As long as you live I will love you, and I will wait for you, but I will help you free Sabine first, and then I will leave you."

"Joslyn." I breathed her name, recognizing the gift she was offering me. How sweet a girl she was, even still. *Too sweet for Satan,* I thought. *Surely.* "How did you get back here?"

"These passages run underground, all throughout the city. Just before the sun rose, I took shelter in a storeroom. In the cellar was a passage and then another. Eventually, they led me to the Grange aux Dimes, and to you." She turned back to face me and I saw her eyes linger on the musculature of my chest, on the ugly scars that crossed it like a crucifix. She shivered, but whether from desire or pity I could not tell.

"And Sabine?" I asked. "You think you know where she is? I ... I ... an island..." I was at a loss to explain my dream of the night before. I had been tired, bereft; perhaps it had been my imagination playing tricks.

"Yes. Far to the south-east of here, there is an isle, the Île de Ré. It is a walled city, a fortress near impenetrable. Once before Beltran has taken me there—a bloody place surrounded by a great wall. Beltran had been there to feed on the corpses of the carnage following the siege of 1627. Afterwards, he told me, the king had commissioned a master engineer, Vauban, to build the wall and citadel. At the time, men said no place in France was better defended and that sixteen thousand people could be protected there for a year or more."

And what place made by man could ward off an attack by Vampires? I thought.

"Beltran has many such places around the globe, but this is the most well-defended. I believe he will have taken her there. But what did Gandler mean by her blood debt?" Joslyn picked up my shirt where I had discarded it on the floor, patted the creases smooth, and threw it to me.

I reached up and caught it, slipped it on. "He had a son: Fritz. It was Sabine's job to guard the boy. Gandler threatened her, of course. The boy had a blood disorder. He made more blood than required and bled from the eyes, nose, mouth. From most of his orifices. A tasty morsel for Vampire. When they killed him, Gandler blamed Sabine."

Joslyn looked puzzled. "But she is immortal, is she not?"

"Yes. But there are still ways to end a Sphinx's eternity." With trembling hands, I picked up the incunabulum from where it lay on the floor. I had read it only cursorily, once, hundreds of years before when I had given it to Joslyn.

"Every night, she returns to the place from whence she came: her anchorstone," I explained as I flipped through the pages. The sheets were thinner than I remembered all those years ago, and worn, the color faded from them. "She will tell no one where it is, not even me. Destroying it is the only way to kill her. Gandler has searched for it for decades. When he finds it, he will grind it into dust, and with it Sabine."

"And until then..." Joslyn asked.

"He will torture her. Nightly will he destroy her, and daily will she vanish to her stone, only to return at moonrise completely renewed. I can only imagine how that will frustrate Gandler. It will amuse him and Beltran to think up new tortures for her."

Joslyn drew in her breath.

With a heavy heart, I turned to the page about the Sphinx and began to read:

"A mythological hybrid, the Sphinx is a beautiful woman with the wings of an eagle and the supple body of a lion, although several other variations of this creature have been observed. From whence such mysterious creatures arise it is hard to say, but they exist in countless mythologies and in various incantations, and literature and art are rife with representations of this preternatural beast."

I cringed at the word, knowing how Sabine would hate to be described so, and then read on:

"Grecian Sphinxes are known to have the head and breasts of a woman, the wings of an eagle and the body of a lioness, and the name Sphinx is indeed derived from the Greek. Egyptian sphinxes, many of which are male, are known as 'shesep-ankh,' a name that translates loosely as 'living image,' perhaps a reference to the Sphinx's affiliation with lifelike sculpture. Immortal, and sometimes immoral, this magical creature is tenacious, resilient, ferocious, and associated with a single stone or statue that appears to anchor the creature to the earthly realm and is said to confine it by day. It is said that Sphinxes are able to choose a new stone by night by roaring before the desired sculpture beneath a full moon. If no roar answers back, the stone is otherwise unoccupied and the Sphinx might enter it and bind herself to it. However, Sphinxes are known to be highly territorial and will fight for the right to a particular stone if already occupied, which leads this author to assert that few leave their anchorstones voluntarily. Further mythology has it that a Sphinx can be woken from the anchorstone by day, and there have been reports of a Sphinx's eyes suddenly snapping open to vigilantly watch the area under his or her protection. Some suggest a kiss, or a spell, the words of which have never been adequately relayed to this author, may partially rouse a Sphinx by day. Perhaps unsurprisingly, tombs and temples appear to be the haunts of this mysterious creature, which is active only by night and entirely absent by day. Sphinxes feed on meat or carrion but may also dine upon Vampires, although this cataloguer finds such suggestion doubtful. Lifespan and reproductive history are unknown, but it appears only the destruction of the stone results in the Sphinx's ultimate end."

Although there was no mention of the riddle, the words gave me some comfort. I stroked the page, which bore a stylized golden figure of a Sphinx. She must have changed her stone, I realized, perhaps several times since she had guarded Ramesses' tomb. Gandler did not have the stone, and the book had made no mention of the riddle, so Sabine's suffering was, at least, temporary. Then, thinking of the hours I had spent searching for her stone in Paris and realizing it might be anywhere, I handed the book back to Joslyn, disappointed.

"This fortress, the Île de Ré," I asked. "Is there any way to breach the fortifications? What weapons are there, and where are they situated? If I am able to fly in, where can I land with safety? Where inside do you think they might keep her?"

"The defensives are many. Even with an army, we might struggle to gain entry. And if we do, how will you defeat so many of them?"

Sabine's words in my dream—*an army of undead*—rang

in my ears. "An army we do not have." I sighed. "Although they do."

The task seemed insurmountable. Why? I silently accused my Maker. Why make me like this, a solitary killer with no army to operate against the undead? Such hatred for them and myself their only weapon. It rankled me. I felt I had been set an impossible task, one I could only hope to fail in perpetuity, as I had failed to protect Joslyn all those centuries ago, as I had failed to protect Sabine just days hence. A roar of anger issued from me and I slapped my ruined wings in disgust.

"What is it?" Joslyn's lip trembled.

"Nothing but that the world seems too unfair. How is it Beltran and Gandler, and beasts of their kind, can live, but Danette and Sabine and you and I must suffer so? How is it that, for all I do for God, he punishes me thus?"

"Do not talk of God." Joslyn shivered, and I suddenly noticed the torn white silk had been replaced with the dress of a noblewoman: green silk taffeta with embroidered Chinoiserie flowers. A droplet of blood stained the bodice. I tried to contain a shiver of disgust.

"I wondered, once, why he never spoke to me all of those years ago in the convent," Joslyn said. "But now I realize that neither of them do, at least not in words, only in deed." She smoothed down the full petticoats. "I do not hear Satan's forked tongue whispering, but nor do I hear your Maker's harps ever playing for me. All that was holy and good in me I gave away for you. You were the only god I prayed to, and prayed for, my guardian angel. And now, all there is left for me is to believe in you and to protect you."

I wanted to weep at that, for if only I had protected her that night, we would not be here with my senses acutely aware of her every movement and her tear-stained eyes avoiding my gaze. But then she would be long dead. Bones in a grave. The thought chilled me.

"I do not hear him either," I admitted. "Perhaps God is mute, or I have already failed him and his silence is my punishment."

"No," Joslyn said, and her eyes filled again with tears. "He has failed you."

The Île de Ré was south-east some three hundred and forty miles. Even had I been able to fly that far on my injured wings, Joslyn could not. If we could procure a horse and buggy, the journey would take us a week or more, but animals were known to baulk at preternatural masters, potentially extending our journey. More worrying, for me, was whether I could be alone with her for so long? Traveling by day presented us with further problems and would require Joslyn to be concealed in a casket in a covered wagon, so we conceived upon the idea that I was an undertaker, carrying a noblewoman's body to her father in La Rochelle.

After our preparations, we both slept deeply: myself curled away to face the wall and Joslyn in an alcove near the entrance to our chamber. I knew from her face that she longed to curl into me, but even asleep I was a threat to her.

It was close to midnight before we awoke, so tired were we from the emotions of the night before.

"Come," I told her. "You must feed, and so must I." I had hoped that keeping myself sated might prevent me from desiring her. "Go!" I commanded. "And meet me back here within three hours, whence we will take our leave. If I am late returning, it will be because I must find a carriage that can bear us, and a casket to contain you."

"A nice one," she instructed.

"Go!"

Glad as I had been to see her this morning, I was almost as relieved when she left. After ten minutes or so, I stole out after her. The streets were quiet. Only the smell of the markets lingered. Where might I find blood to nourish me on a night like this? I thought. Perhaps I would not. Unless ... had some of them returned to seek me out or to find Joslyn? It was all I could hope for. For hours, I prowled the shadows and loitered in the poplar groves. My nostrils twitched for just a sniff of Vampire blood, but they had all vanished. I contented myself with finding a carriage for our journey. If I were to play the part of an undertaker, I reasoned, I might as well be authentic. The smell of brine and embalming fluid led me to the mortuary. There, in the stables, was a horse-drawn hearse and the sturdy black mare that pulled it. It would be a conspicuous theft, no doubt, but I figured few would argue once they saw me, and Joslyn and I would be long gone on the road to the Île de Ré by the time the mortician had arisen.

Perhaps I should have brought her with me, to ensure he would not arise. The thought was absurd and immoral. A bitter laugh sprang from me.

"You laugh?"

I spun, unsettled by my unexpected companion.

"Joslyn! You must leave me."

"You have not yet fed?"

"It is not so easy for one such as I. My prey is less unassuming than yours." My words were harsh to her ears I could tell, but I could not keep the accusation from my tone.

"Feed on me again. You did not kill me last time."

"Joslyn!" I said her name like an obscenity. "It must never happen again."

"You have a horse, I see. And a carriage. Now for a coffin." She wisely changed the subject.

"Keep watch," I instructed her. "I will return in good time."

As I had expected, the mortician locked his doors, but I flew over the walled garden and inspected the stone building until I found a high window I thought was not properly latched. On tender wings, I flapped up to the window and carefully nudged open the shutters, slipping inside as quietly as a zephyr. Downstairs, in the deathly quiet of the parlor, a body had been laid out. I could hear the faint wheeze of the mortician's snores upstairs and the ticking of a timepiece as I approached the cedar casket. The body was covered with a pall and wreathed with champagne roses—a coffin for a woman. After moving the flowers, I folded back the pall and gasped. The eyes of the flower seller sprang open. "My Lord," she said, as she sat up in her coffin.

Horror twisted my guts, but she looked around vacantly and then flung her arms around me. "E said he'd come back for me, tho' he weren't nearly as beautiful as you are, my angel," she said. "I knew you'd come for me. Come, give Bessie a kiss."

As she held her face up and pursed her lips, I knew immediately what she was, and who had made her this. "Beltran," I whispered and sank my teeth deep into her throat.

When I had finished and she was dead for the second time, I propped her in a chair in the corner. There was little I could do to relieve the mortician of his surprise.

"He is turning so many these days."

I nearly jumped as high as the mortician might have at seeing the flower seller's body newly risen from her casket.

"Joslyn!" I had been so engrossed in my task that I had not heard her approach.

"So many bodies." She gestured to the flower seller. "Any he can find and turn in time."

"Yes." I nodded grimly. "And how should we defeat this growing army of corpses?"

Joslyn looked sorrowful. "I wish I knew."

"You have fed?"

"Yes."

Once more revulsion gripped me. "Let us away. Is the casket to your satisfaction?"

Joslyn ran a hand over the satin lining. "Yes, I think it will do."

"Good. Help me get it through the window."

"Wait," said Joslyn, when we had the coffin concealed within the carriage. She slipped back inside. When she returned some minutes later, her lips were crimson with blood and she carried a small parcel.

"The mortician?" I asked, and revulsion flooded me.

"Yes. And his wife."

"And the parcel?" I tried to keep the disgust from my voice.

Joslyn bent her head, and I saw then the instruments she had taken.

Holding aloft the syringe of her own blood, she said, "You must keep up your strength; this worked once before."

I shivered. "It will never be enough."

"It will be better than nothing."

THIRTEEN

We had gone not seven miles before a scene on the road ahead forced us to slow. When we drew closer, I made out the vibrant caravans of Gandler's former Circus of Curiosities. My immediate instinct was to turn and flee, but to do so would cost us time—time we had not and time that could mean Sabine's life.

"What if Gandler has returned?" I pondered aloud.

"To this motley bunch? He no longer needs them." Joslyn crept up beside me. I wished she hadn't. It was too close, too much of a distraction.

"He has what he was seeking."

"Yes, and he has Sabine as well."

"Perhaps they might help us? We cannot travel far with just one mare and no others to rest her, and they have ponies and oxen to spare now there are fewer wagons."

I considered her words. "I wonder why they did not split up? Take their chances."

"Trudie cannot even stand, let alone walk, and Seamus and Sinbad would no doubt struggle. No, they need someone to take care of them."

"Or to exploit them."

Joslyn gave a near imperceptible nod. "Yes, or that. Come, let us talk to them. At the very least, they should be grateful."

As our mare trotted closer, I noted that the scarred boy, Kettle's son Kellane, was leading the small caravan.

"Oh-ho and what have we here?" he cried when I drew close enough for him to recognize me.

"Kellane, I am surprised you haven't left to pursue your freedom or your fortune."

"What makes you think I haven't? We're leaving, aren't we?" He scratched at one of the scars that marred his otherwise jovial face.

"I suppose so. And Trudie and the twins?"

"They're leaving with us. We could hardly just leave them there. Besides, who's to say we can't make a fortune from this? After all, we have Giselle, and Lee and me'll give them all a tidy slice of the profits. And who knows who or what we might meet on the road to Tours? Maybe a few more exhibits."

"Like an angel and a Vampire queen," I heard one of the twins say—Seamus, I thought it was—as a wagon lurched past on my right.

"It is a shame about the lioness, though," Sinbad said.

"That's enough," I growled. "So you are headed south-east, to Tours?"

"Yes, and you?"

I wondered again whether they might be trusted. "To the Île de Ré."

Lee's eyebrows danced at that and he threw his brother a knowing glance. "Île de Ré? What on earth might you want there?"

"Vengeance."

Kellane's expression grew wary. "Might be I'd join you, if

your adversary is who I think it is?"

"No. I must do this alone. Your father would have wanted you to stay safe. To protect Giselle."

"My father," Kellane said, "is the reason I have these scars, the reason Giselle is as she is, a miserable, frightened dwarf girl. My father, bless his departed soul"—he crossed himself—"was a man not brave enough to fight his oppressors, too cowardly to seek his vengeance."

"Your father was no such thing. You have your freedom. Use it wisely, Kellane, not just for you, but for Giselle and these others."

"Ways I sees it, freedom is just another word for unemployed. Wouldn't you agree, Sinbad?" came the voice from the covered wagon.

"Or for hungry," Trudie joined them. "And I am. How hungry I am, Kell. Couldn't I have just a bite of bread? Just a nip of wine or a nibble of cheese? Please, please. I'm so famished. I might starve here if you cannot spare me a pittance."

"It will be a cold day in hell when you starve to death," Seamus taunted her.

"Be quiet, or I will feed you to her," Kellane told him, and it struck me that everything was as it had always been. Gandler's Circus of Curiosities would carry on as it had before, even without him.

"If you really want your vengeance," I changed the subject, "there is a way you can help."

"I'm listening."

"We have only one horse. If you can spare us some ponies or oxen we might make better time."

"And we should give you these ponies because…?" Lee stepped forward.

"For this." Joslyn held up the bag she had taken from the mortician's house and jangled it. "For gold."

"I have a better idea," said Kellane. "We will keep our

horses, but we will let you have use of them until we reach Tours, in exchange for two things."

My skin crawled with the feeling I knew what he might ask, and Joslyn's already pale face grew whiter. I drew in a breath. "What might that be?"

"Protection."

I exhaled with a sigh of relief.

"Protection by night from her and all of her kind." Lee pointed to Joslyn.

"She means you no harm," I told him.

"No, but Gandler might."

"And the other thing?"

"Let us exhibit you by day. I'll give you half of what the townspeople will pay to see a real live angel and a Vampire."

We arrived at Tours within the week, having made good time regularly swapping the mare with the ponies and oxen from Gandler's circus. By then, my nerves had been whittled away by the nearness of Joslyn and the constant bickering of Sinbad and Seamus, combined with Trudie's incessant wheedling and pleading for food. No doubt, Kellane and Lee had the same misgivings. Surprisingly, our journey's swiftness was also aided by the distinct absence of Vampires, a fact that both perplexed and troubled me. Had Beltran really relinquished his grasp on Joslyn for good? Somehow I doubted it, but it worried me what else might have employed Gandler and Beltran to prevent them seeking me out. What horrors awaited Sabine that had made them too busy to goad me?

Sometimes, still on the cusp of evening, we saw shadowy wings above the vineyards as we approached Tours, but they never came close enough to trouble us. Few on the road threatened us either, although many of the townsfolk came, coin in hand, to see us. We put on a good show for them. Joslyn, dressed in finery, looked more ethereally regal than any queen, but it was me that most came to ogle. Some crossed themselves and others left oaten honeycakes or rosary beads, but all of them looked more pious than alarmed, which surprised me after my confinement in the tower.

At Tours, we were to part, and I could tell that Kellane and Lee were nervous about it. Not because they required our protection, but because Joslyn and I were still drawing spectators.

"We shall be sorry to see you leave," Kellane told me as I unhitched the last two piebald ponies and replaced the harness on the old black mare.

"You should find some other employ." I moved cautiously around the animal. Although usually calm with me, she had come to hate Joslyn and would shy and whinny whenever she approached. "This business of exhibiting freaks, no good can come of it."

"And do what? Beg in the streets? Pick pockets?"

"Anything," I urged. "Anything but this. Look at her." I pointed to Trudie's wagon. The locks had all been removed, but it was still a cage.

"Her fat traps her, not I."

"We are all trapped by something." I climbed back up onto the wagon.

"Aye. That we are. And we all set traps for others. Tell me, what trap do you intend to set for Gandler, and do you know what deceit you're walking into? The Île de Ré is the best-defended place in all of France. How do you think an angel and one lone, miserable female Vampire can possibly defeat him?"

"Because I have something he does not." I slid the leather reins through my hands, drawing them up.

"Balls." Kellane laughed at his own joke.

"No. Faith."

He put his scarred head to the side. "So it is true then, Feathers. You really do have God on your side."

"I hope so."

"Here." The moon hung like a golden fruit in the sky as Joslyn roused herself and joined me at the reins. I could feel her presence before I could see her, could smell her blood; it always seemed infused with rosemary, or was it just my imagination? She handed me a syringe, blood-dark in the twilight, and I licked my lips.

"Let me," she said. She rolled up my sleeve and slid the syringe into my vein, emptying the chamber slowly.

It was never enough, but it had sustained me on our journey, and each night my longing for it was sharper than for laudanum. Each time, she smiled as she watched her blood color my cheeks, and my eyes close slightly at the needle's bite. It was as if she were satisfied with even this, as if this bound us intimately together, and I suppose it did. Mostly, though, her intimacy was still too much for me, her nearness too raw. When she retreated to the casket to sleep, I let the meditative clop of hooves lull me and freed myself from the bonds of loving her. But nothing, not even the blood or the dulling effect of the moonlight frosting the vines, could lessen the hatred of Beltran and Gandler that blackened my heart or reduce my fear and longing for Sabine.

As I drove the horses onward, I considered how we might gain access to St Martin de Re, Beltran's stronghold. Of course, the city was walled, but if my wings healed quickly we might breach them, or, at least, I might. Many times I had cursed to myself knowing that Joslyn, even as she knew Beltran's mind, would be naught but a liability. I had enough to concern myself with regarding Sabine. I did not need to have to protect Joslyn as well. I wondered how I might convince her to remain in La Rochelle, yet I knew she would never let me go to the island without her. Several times I thought back to the night in Gandler's tent. How she had seemingly betrayed me, promised to hand Sabine to Gandler. Was I certain she could be trusted? Then I remembered the blue-eyed child with her arms outstretched, the young woman who loved passionfruit, and the bat that had clung to my breast, and I scolded myself for my suspicion.

I hired a small skiff when we reached La Rochelle, and we made our approach to the Île de Ré by night, alighting on the beach south of the port and wearing the garb of fisherfolk, clothes which Joslyn had returned with on one of her nightly forays. I did not ask what had happened to the clothing's owners. I already knew, and the thought disgusted me. How could I love what she had become? Her blood seemed to suck like a parasite in my veins. Yet I loved and craved her as much as ever.

Turning from her, I looked around. Already my skin crawled with the place. I could feel them there, everywhere, and a dread excitement thinned my blood. It became immediately clear how impossible a task we had set ourselves. High ramparts with star-shaped sentry points surrounded the city.

"How do you plan on gaining access to the stronghold?" Joslyn asked. Her look was of fear, but not for herself. Her eyes flew to my damaged right wing.

She fears for me.

"I shall have to fly in. The walls are too high for me to scale without detection." I pointed out the cannon that protruded from the walls. "You stay here. You have come far enough." I stared at the walled city.

"No." The force of her words turned my head. "I will not leave you. It might be I have a better idea. Let me go to them willingly and profess my contrition and my love for Beltran.

It is all he has ever wanted to hear from me. They will take me straight to him, and when I find out where Sabine is, I will get a message to you. Perhaps smoke or fire or a din."

I raised my eyebrows, and she glanced at my burned wings again. "Poor, Ame," she said tenderly. "I suppose you have had enough of smoke and fire."

No, it is you who should be pitied for them, Joslyn, I thought. *You will have your fill of them in hell.*

"I will not let you go in there, will not let you go to him defenseless. You heard him. What if his words were true? If he does not want you, you might be walking to a death sentence. Then what would I have? I would have lost you both. No. It is unworkable."

"Ame." She put her hand on my arm, but I shrugged her off. "You still do not trust me?"

I looked away, at the slow-lapping water of the Breton Strait.

"If I should do this, then we can fight them together: you, me, and Sabine. There are hundreds of them, Gandler and Beltran besides. How do you hope to free her alone? You would be flying to your death."

"And yet you would gladly hurry towards yours? No. I cannot let you."

Joslyn sat in the sand and drew her legs up to her chest. "Without you, I would gladly rush to death. I have begged you for it. If you leave me here, I will go to them anyway. I will try to fight for you, and they will imprison me and leave me to burn most horribly at daybreak. They may well make you watch. Then you will have lost everything. Sabine, me, your life. Gandler knows your secrets now, remember."

"Thanks to you." I did not tell her that I was unsure whether such an injection would even work. Perhaps a Cruxim had to kill a mortal to die that way. I felt frustration mounting in me again at knowing so little, and I clenched my teeth.

Joslyn obviously mistook my expression for anger. "I had thought you would kill him then and there. That he would taste sweet to you after what he had done to Sabine and that poor girl Danette. I did not know he would live on to confirm your weakness to Beltran."

"No matter. What is done is done. He knows; they both know." I did not tell her that Beltran had suspected as much anyway. Did not tell her about the pitiful mortal girl Beltran had once claimed to be her. "I shall not rest until I have exterminated them all."

Joslyn stood again and came to me. "Ame, this is the only way. Please, let me try this. I will not wait out here for you to die without me."

I sighed, considering. "One condition."

"Yes."

"As soon as you are inside, at your earliest opportunity, you find a way to alert me and to let me in to wherever they hold Sabine. I will fly in over the ramparts if I can, but I need to know where she is. Where do you think is a likely place for them to keep her?"

Joslyn frowned. "I have been here but once before, but I hope for her sake it is the Eglise St Martin and not the citadel."

"And if it is the citadel?"

"Then we will need an army."

I sighed and ran a hand through my hair. "Either way we would need an army. This is foolishness."

"No, Ame." Joslyn's voice was quiet and sad in the darkness. "This is love."

I thought of Sabine's warm body curled against mine, of hunting beside her, her fierce hatred for my enemy. Of how she had gone to Joslyn, her jealousy and hatred aside, to save me. The thought of the deprivations Gandler might visit on her spurred me on.

"Then so be it. Go, but when you are in, I shall fly to you

once you can give me a sign."

"But what sign?" Joslyn paced the beach. "Smoke will surely give me away. It must be something you will recognize by sight from a distance."

"Joslyn." It came to me in an instant. "The incunabulum. Its gilt cover will glow in the sunlight by day when all else are abed. Take it with you. Tell them it is a gift you are returning to Gandler. But then, by night, leave it out somewhere for me on a ledge or a turret where it will catch the morning sun. I will fly over the city by day, trying to find you, and when I see it, I will know you and Sabine are there." My mind added, *And hopefully still alive.*

Just before the sun had risen, Joslyn had drawn out a syringe-full of her blood and injected it into me. Then she had marched towards the gates of the walled city. Concealed beneath the skiff, I watched her go. Her usual bearing, proud and strong, became defeated and weak as she made her way up to the square gatehouse, holding the incunabulum before her. I knew that the sentinels in the entrance were not mere men. Perhaps by day they were human, but by night, each would know who she was: a supplicant Vampire come to beg her Lord for forgiveness. Screeches and laughter followed her conversation with the guardsmen, although I could not hear what she said. When two of them leaped down to her, grasping her roughly, she pulled her arm away before relenting and letting them lead her through the gates. Just before the vaulted doors closed behind her, she glanced over her shoulder once more. This time, the fear in her eyes was for herself.

I cursed silently. What terrible mistake had I made?

I worried on it until the sun colored the Breton Strait and the waves washed away my troubles and gave me an uninterrupted hour or two of sleep. When I woke, it was to the funk of seaweed and salt-air trapped beneath the skiff.

I lifted the boat to look out. Seeing nothing, I flipped the skiff over and stood. My wings ached, my entire body ached, but none more than my heart. Joslyn and Sabine, both in the walled city, and me out here sleeping on a beach. I cursed myself again and set off in the direction of the wall, trying to avoid the sections where a parapet or guard tower topped the ramparts.

After another hour, when the sun was higher in the sky, I found a place where a hillock and a tree made the height of the wall slightly less formidable. A slight rise hid the position a little from the nearest guard tower. If I could flutter up into the tree's branches to rest, and then on to the top of the wall, I might have the strength in my wings to make it down the other side. If I did not, the fall was not too great. If they saw me, I had no doubt cannonfire would result.

My wing strength was returning slowly, and each shot of Joslyn's blood had helped, but although she had been gone just hours, already I craved more.

Please, I prayed to whomever it was that might hear a Cruxim's prayers. *Please let her find Sabine. Soon.*

I decided to fly over the walls in the late afternoon, just before sunset, and conceal myself somewhere inside for the night, hoping I might be able to catch an unwary Vampire that night to enhance my strength. Tomorrow, my wings must be good enough to fly over the city, searching for the gleam of gold that would reveal the whereabouts of my two dearest loves and my two greatest enemies. No doubt, as night fell, hordes of bats would fly out from the castle in search of me. Beltran was no fool. As much as he would want to believe that Joslyn had returned for him, that she had seen the error of her ways and loved him, he would still have them hunt for me. It struck me that he and Gandler would love nothing more than to force her to kill me herself to prove her love for Beltran. Or Sabine, the thought suddenly struck me. What might they make her do to Sabine? After all, surely Gandler had realized the two had worked together to destroy him.

My brain was numb with thoughts of losing them both by the time the sun began to dip toward the land. Testing my wings, I gingerly flapped up into the tree and perched there like a bird momentarily, waiting for the dull pain in my wings to either worsen or dissipate. It faded faster than I had hoped: a good sign. With a further flap, I was on the wall. I had not been seen. Without waiting this time, I launched myself off the stone and felt my wings coast me down to the ground on the other side. It had gone better than I had hoped. Now to find a place to conceal myself before the sentries began to make their rounds. I approached the nearest building and found a chink in the edifice to pull myself up the stone. *Quickly, quickly,* I cautioned myself. The roof was no good. Despite the old sayings, bats have good eyesight. No, somewhere inside, or by a window ledge, or perhaps even behind drapery would be better, or an alcove where I could conceal myself for a time in a place that was infrequently used.

I continued to pull myself up the wall until I came to a section where the flintstone grew rougher, and I spied a window ledge above. The window was shuttered, but the next along showed a small chink of light. Perhaps, if I could hover long enough, I could work it open. What I might find on the other side was the question.

Pulling myself up to just below the window, I put my ear to the cold stone. I could hear nothing at first, then a low murmuring and the staccato of footprints moving away. I inched further up the wall, grasping the thicker window ledge now, and put one hand up to tug at the shutters. They were barred, but loosely, as if not quite fastened. I listened again. Nothing. Moving my weight off the wall and onto my wings, I fluttered up. It was a bearable pain and one I thought

I could endure for several minutes if I had to. I rattled the window again. Still shuttered. Bearing the weight of one leg on the windowsill, and thankful for the drab colors of my fisherfolk garb, which blended in with the dappled gray of the wall, I kicked the shutters inward with all of my might, splintering one and breaking the hinge on the other, sending it dangling. Without hesitation, I dropped back down to the window ledge and leaped inside.

The room was not empty. A shriek rang out as a black-haired Vampire, who had clearly just arisen from a draped four-poster bed, sprang for me. From behind the floral silk that garlanded the bed, I could see another creature stir. I rushed at the first without a sound. Grabbing his long black hair in hand, I jerked his head to the side and my fangs met his jugular, forcing him to his knees, his shriek a dying gurgle as his strength ebbed into me.

"Giordano...?" came a woman's voice, still thick with sleep.

I slid back the draped silk a little and peered in. A titian-haired woman lay on her side, her back to me. Still half asleep, she patted the bed behind her with one hand, searching for her mate.

"Shhh," I said softly and reached out so she could feel my hand. Her hand was icy, and I noticed the line of fang-shaped welts along her neck. She had recently been mortal, too, this one, but no more. My weight sliding into bed reassured her, and she murmured and gripped my hand but did not turn over. Carefully, I moved close to her and lifted a strand of red hair from her creamy neck. She did not say a word, and she died so quickly, encircled in my arms.

I might have felt sorry for the deception, had she not been what she was. Still, filling as they were, I enjoyed it less than I had Joslyn's daily administrations.

Their deaths enriched me, but even with a skinful

of Vampire blood, I was no match for Beltran and his henchmen, and now I had bodies to hide. Late risers they were, but no doubt someone would come to miss Giordano and his lover eventually. No, I had to stuff them somewhere. If only it had been nearly sunrise instead of close to dusk and I might have tossed them out the window and let the sun and wind reduce their bodies to ashes.

A wooden trunk sat at the bed end and looked as if it might be large enough to house them both. I emptied it of the jumble of clothes and linen, keeping only a shirt and trousers that appeared they might fit and kicking the rest under the bed. After I had forced the corpses in, I regretted the decision; the trunk would have made a good place to hide. However, I wanted to put some distance between myself and my kills, should they be missed.

The trousers and shirt fit, so I crossed the room and took a hat and cloak off the stand near the heavy oak door. I peered out into the hallway.

There seemed to be no one about. Not yet, but I was still wary. I snuck out of the room and down to the staircase. Craning my neck, I looked down it. Nothing. There was no one on the staircase coming from above either, so I made the decision to ascend. Higher would be better in the morning, when I flew out to look for Joslyn's signal. After listening in the hall for movement beyond and finding it empty, I entered a room at the end. It was less sumptuously decorated, looking almost like a governess's quarters, and had a vacant air. Thick, dark drapes concealed the window and made the room unnaturally dark. I shut myself away in the closet, buried beneath a coverlet, and tried to sleep.

Daybreak brought with it screams from a room further down the hall. Was this entire city a nest of bloodsuckers? Clearly a Vampire on this floor was playing with his supper. Would their cruelty never end? Ignoring the swelling hatred inside me, I crept from my hiding place and pulled back the drapes. The sun was not yet fully risen. Soon, its rays would be strong enough to reveal what I was looking for: the glint of gold on gray. Until then, I may as well keep up my strength. Every death was one less Vampire in the army of them I knew I would face when I located Joslyn and Sabine. It occurred to me that I no longer distinguished between the two of them. Much as I knew that Joslyn had to die, the daily injections of her blood had both fuelled and quelled my need for her. *She needs to be saved,* I thought, *as much as Sabine. Only from herself and her kind.* Yet I knew that only He could save her.

I left the sanctity of my room and stole down the hall, following the symphony of screams. When I grew closer, the screams turned to pleading. A girl's voice. Cowards— they so often preyed on the weak. When I pushed open the door, I saw three of them, all men, holding down a girl of about seventeen, taking turns at her throat as she sobbed and begged for mercy.

"My turn," one said and nudged another off her.

"No! Mine!" I sprang at him. With a surge of strength, I grasped his head and banged it full force into the skull of the Vampire that clambered over her body. It was enough to concuss both for a moment while I took care of their friend, draining him in seconds.

"Sharing, were we?" I asked as I punched the first man—a blue-eyed, sharp-nosed, blood-spattered creature—in the mouth and then dined on him too, pinning him to the bed behind the girl, whose screams had intensified so much I worried she might bring someone running.

"Shhh." I held one finger up to my bloodied lips. "You're not my type."

The third Vampire leaped back to his feet. His shirt off and his trousers still unbuckled, he sprang at me with a hiss. The girl's blood stained his mouth, and as he wiped at it with one hand, I kicked out, striking his kneecap and dropping him to the ground.

"You, on the other hand," I said and delivered a blow to his mouth that snapped one of his fangs. It skittered off across the room. Impressed by how quickly their blood had strengthened me, I bit down hard into his shoulder. He struggled, but I put my hand over his mouth and nose, until he, too, went limp.

The girl, still on her back, scrabbled away from me. White showed around her terrified eyes.

"All will be well," I told her, as I wondered what to do about her. If she ran out there babbling, Beltran and Gandler were sure to have their minions find me in no time. Yet I had no way of keeping her in here either, and her face told me that she bore me no love for killing her attackers. No doubt she, like countless others, considered me one of them. In the end, I did the only thing I could do: I revealed my wings. Bedraggled as they were, when I flapped them I was surprised to find them fanned out around me, replete with new-growing feathers. My strength was returning, more suddenly than I had imagined.

"I am an angel of the Lord," I lied to her. "Go now, little one, and spread the word of His light, but tell no one you have seen me lest they call you a liar. The Lord loves you. As they brought you darkness"—I gestured to the dead Vampires—"He brings you light. Now, hurry." I pointed to the door.

Clutching her torn dress, she ran and did not look back.

When she had gone, I opened the window again. The sun had fully risen. Pulling the drapes all the way open, I opened the window and tossed the bodies out one by one. They speckled to gray ash as the sunlight struck them and made no impression against the stone edifice. When I had hurled the last one out, and the sun had begun to scale the blue heavens, I launched myself out too. Power, exhilarating power, coursed through me. I am stronger than they. I smiled, feeling like myself for the first time since my escape from Sezanne tower. The thought gave me hope. Wheeling east on my recovered wings, I soared over the city of St Martin de Re.

I had nearly given up, when I finally saw it: the faint glint of something on a ledge down near the ruined church of St Martin. My soul sang for Joslyn. *You have offered me far more than I ever offered you.* I had wronged her in many ways, and she in just one: Beltran. If only he had not been there that night.

I swooped down closer to look. Yes! There it was. She had set the book on the body of a gargoyle that jutted out from a turret.

I longed to swoop down immediately and enter the church, but I knew that where Joslyn was, Beltran and his allies would be too. I would not let him escape this time. I had to be cautious. Down there, I would be even more exposed than I was up here, flying in the sunshine in broad daylight. Instead, I fluttered down onto the gargoyle, picked up the book, and stared in through the stone archway.

As I had expected, I could see nothing inside the darkened church. By day, they would be sleeping, or at least most of them, but there would surely be sentries. So far, my incursion into the walled city had been too easy. Were they watching me, awaiting the moment to capture me, or was there a host of guards inside who would bar my way? I guessed the latter. Mumbled voices came from below, moans and whimpers, as if someone were in pain.

Sabine, I thought, and then realized it could not be her. It was day; she would be absent unless Gandler had found her anchorstone.

Joslyn? Grabbing the ledge above, I hauled myself in through the window. A shiver gripped me at entering a tower so like the one I had recently escaped at Sezanne, but the thought of Sabine and Joslyn made me press on. I followed the voices to a stone antechamber. Carefully, my body pressed to the wall, I peeked in. Sleeping Vampires hung from the ceiling, cocooned in their cloaks. More slumbered on the floor, folded into each other's arms. In sleep, they were beautiful, limbs entwined, some curled into each other like a litter of sleek kittens. Elegant as they were, a bitter taste filled my mouth, a dry longing that preceded the darkness of my rage: my need for their deaths. I wanted to rush in headlong and destroy them one by one, but even I could see that would be pointless. There were too many, forty at least.

Controlling my bloodlust, I searched for Joslyn. She was not there. Not among them. How could that be when the incunabulum was here for me? A great weariness gripped me. She had to be here! She would never have left it for me otherwise. I searched the faces of the sleeping Vampires again, one by one. She was not there.

Whimpering distracted me again, and I turned to make out a cage set in the corner of the room. Crammed into it were several young men and women, all of them pale with blood loss. Three sleepy-looking Vampires stood by them, brandishing a sword. I took a step backward, bile rising into my throat. It would never do for them to see me.

Still searching the room, I noticed that while neither Joslyn nor Sabine were there, nor were Gandler or Beltran. I backed into the hallway to consider my options. If I rushed in there now, I might kill the sentries and twenty or so of the sleeping Vampires. But even if I were stealthy enough to kill most of them while they slumbered, the mortals would surely give me away. If Joslyn were here somewhere, I might save her, but Sabine, if indeed she were still alive at all, would still be captive. And Beltran and Gandler would still be at large.

Drawing attention to myself would also expose Joslyn's

lies. No, better to wait, to think of another way to find them, and to save them. Quickly, I backed out the way I had come, the sunshine a welcome respite from the grim room.

Stuffing the incunabulum under my shirt, I inched along the chequered flint and sandstone wall to the next window. The next room was empty, and the next, but the street below was beginning to wake. In despair, I dove from the window ledge and flew quickly back down onto the street.

With the hat tugged low on my brow, I put on my coat to conceal my wings, placed the gilt book into my pocket, and examined the Eglise de St Martin from every angle, running my hand over the sandstone walls, peering in the windows on the lower floors. The church, the vestry, and the small temple beyond all seemed empty; the only presence was of death. I could smell it loitering in the high, vaulted ceilings. If this church had ever been a place of God, it was no longer. I wondered what had happened to the parishioners and then remembered the cage in the room above. If there was any sign of Joslyn or Sabine, or a concealed door that might reveal them, I found none. I left disillusioned, filled with rage at them and disgust with myself for having let Joslyn walk into a trap.

I did not fly back to the room that had been my earlier hideout; it was too dangerous. Men were awake now, and I had to conceal myself among them. It seemed as if the men and women I passed in the streets knew that a scourge of the undead filled their city, defiled their churches. No doubt some of the mortals were in their employ, or indeed hoped to join their ranks. *Did they feed here,* I wondered, *or fly out as bats to rid La Rochelle, Aytre and La-Tranche-sur-mer of their inhabitants? Probably the latter,* I considered. As I hurried on, cries rang out from an alley to my right.

"Step away, Mademoiselle, lest you catch it too," a robust, bearded fellow cautioned a woman, who kept flinging herself, distraught, onto the wagon he pulled. I glimpsed bodies stiff with rigor mortis, and on the very top, the corpse of a child, her fair flesh ringed with the red roses of smallpox.

No doubt the pox was feeding them too. Every day, more corpses joined their ranks. I thought of the youth I had tried to catch in Paris on my release from the tower, and I wondered if the vile creatures were turning even innocents into monsters. Keeping my head down, I hurried away from the grieving mother and the pox cart, in search of a safe place to sleep. The silver Lee had paid me from the circus soothed the landlady of a boarding house, Madame Bourret, whose skeptical expression might otherwise have seen me turned away for my pale skin and gleaming teeth. Once inside, I hurried to my room. Sleep evaded me. Why had Joslyn not been there? Where was she? A chill told me she had been there until taken elsewhere. To have left the book, she had to have been forcibly removed. I flipped through the pages, stroking the likely places where her hands had touched. At the page headed Vampire, I stopped to read the entry:

Creatures of the night that feed voraciously on human blood, the Vampire/Vampyre or Nosferatu is a member of the undead risen to life. As guileful as they are beautiful, Vampires are capable of gifting mortal men and women with eternity and are known to frequent many locations throughout Europe and Africa. To turn human beings is recorded as a reciprocal process. The Vampire must first drink from the human, who in turn must drink from the Vampire in order to receive the gift of eternal life. Although likely fanciful, folklore in parts of Eastern Europe ascribes to Vampires the ability to raise a corpse and turn it into a Vampire. Superstitions also have it that plagues of the undead follow pandemics throughout the Continent, and there are indeed reported sightings of Nosferatu following increased incidence of human death.

Although Vampires are considered immortal, "eternal

life" is speculative. Several methods of dispatching Vampires are purportedly effective, including a silver stake through the heart, exposing the creatures to daylight, or forcing them to drink holy water. Vampires are known to be able to take the form of bats, although other shapeshifting behavior is unsubstantiated. There is some belief that other preternatural beings in existence are capable of destroying Vampires by dining upon them, and the Sphinx is believed to be one. Some have suggested the existence of a Vampire-like bounty hunter that nourishes itself on Vampire blood, but this author lacks evidence of a creature with the strength or endurance to fully combat the powerful Vampire.

I snorted. Gifting mortal men and women with eternity. Or damning them to hell.

When I finally slept, it was to nightmares of Joslyn and Sabine both ringed by flames, their dresses catching like incendiaries in the hellfire.

On waking at nightfall, a plan came to me. I left my room and made for the shadows. Not an hour later, I saw one: a pretty, dark-eyed blonde who worked the street. I approached her cautiously, my face still hidden by the hat, and asked her what price I might have to pay.

She laughed bawdily and smoothed a hand down over one shapely hip. "There is a price," she said, "but for a handsome gentleman like you, perhaps I can do a deal."

"I have the gold," I answered and moved closer, as if to embrace her.

She pushed me back. "Monsieur, you must pay first."

My eyes fiery, I put my hands up to her throat and pushed her against the wall. "No, you must. Take me to them, or I will take you to hell."

"I ... I ... I don't know what you mean." Her pupils dilated with recognition of what I was.

My hands were still around her throat. I tightened them.

"You do. Where is Beltran? Where is Gandler?"

Her hands shook as she tried in vain to loosen my grasp on her neck. She coughed and spluttered.

"Scream, or otherwise make a sound, and I will snuff out your eternal life in seconds. Come!" I pulled her back into the alley in the direction of my bedsit, not caring who saw. It was not unusual for a gentleman to consort with ladies of the night, although usually they were mortal. In every city there seemed to be them: Vampire women who turned tricks for victims and were paid in coin and blood. I had often resorted to hunting them.

Back in my room, I pushed her down on the bed and bound her hands with the drawstring from the cheap drapery. One arm subduing her, I leaned over her until my lips were close to her neck and whispered, "Now, tell me what happened to Joslyn?"

I knew what covens were like. I had watched so many over the years. The intrigues. The gossip. The scandals. Every Vampire on this island would be aware of Joslyn's return.

"Beltran ..." she began, choking the words out. Her bosoms heaved under her embroidered corset. A deadly beauty, she might have intoxicated any man but me. "She returned," the woman said. "Joslyn, Beltran's lover."

I must have flinched openly because her eyes widened and she looked amused. "You did not know they were lovers?"

I glanced her neck with my fangs, splitting the skin a little. The closeness of her blood near killed me, but her amusement faded to alarm.

"She said she had been wrong. That she loved Beltran only. She begged his forgiveness."

"I know all this!" I shouted. "Sabine—the Sphinx—is she still alive? Where has he taken her?"

"Y ... Yes," she stammered.

"What has he done to her?"

"Nothing. At least, nothing that lasts. Each day she is whole again and more ferocious than the day before."

It turned my stomach, imagining the horrors visited on her each day anew. Nothing. I did not believe it.

"And Joslyn?"

"Beltran does not trust her." She coughed. "To gain his trust, he said she must bring him you. Must do what she pretended to do last time: to kill you. If not, he will give Joslyn to Gandler too. Another immortal plaything, but one whose scars take longer to heal."

"She does not know where I am," I lied.

"It doesn't matter. They have taken her to the place they keep the Sphinx. If she doesn't tell them..." She shrugged.

It pained me how lightly she took their deaths, or any death. I gritted my teeth and pressed harder on her neck. "Beltran and Gandler? Where do they sleep?"

"The citadel," she said. "They sleep in the citadel."

"Thank you." Then I plunged my teeth into her.

The prostitute's weak groans woke me just before dusk. I had drunk from her to within a heartbeat of satiety; it was not enough. When her heartbeat had become little more than the shudder before death, I forced myself to stop, biting down on my own lip in frustration. Removing her bonnet and cloak, I then bound her.

We had both slept through the day, oblivious to the knocks of the landlady. On awaking, the Vampire had crawled to the door and cowered there, but I did not move to approach her, as much as my body craved more blood.

"What is your name?" I sat up on the bed.

"Evedra." Her brown eyes both feared and hated me.

"Tell me, Evedra, this citadel, what protects it? Lie to me and I will use and discard you. Tell me the truth, and you shall be freed when I have what I came for."

She spat a stream of blood-tinged spittle on the floor near my bed. "Did you come for that traitorous bitch Joslyn, or the Sphinx?"

"Both," I answered, and she laughed mockingly.

"Greedy, Cruxim."

I rushed at her, baring my fangs. "I will show you greed."

Her hands and feet still tied, she cried out and crouched nearer the door.

"But not yet." I sat back on the bed. "Tell me, woman, what I must know. How many Vampires are there? Who leads them? Where are Joslyn and Sabine?"

She sighed. "Say I do. What prevents you from killing me anyway?"

"Because I have great need of you."

Her eyes widened with disgust, and she rubbed at the bites on her neck. "You revolt me."

"The feeling is mutual. Nevertheless, you will help me breach this citadel, and you will take me to Beltran and Gandler. When you do, I will free you."

"You will free me," she mocked. "As if you could. Gandler will torture you, and Beltran will kill you as well as your two sluts when Gandler is finished torturing them and Beltran is tired of raping them."

I flew at her again, snatching her up and feeding some more until, as her heartbeat dulled to the gallop of hooves in the distance, she finally cried out for mercy. It almost felt like a sin to stop, but I wrenched my teeth from her throat and growled, "There are only two mercies I can offer you, wench. The first is to not kill you, and the second, is to. Which will it be?"

"The first. Please, the first," she moaned. "Let me live and I will lead you to Gandler. The man is cruel and a pervert. You may have him."

"And Beltran?"

Her brow furrowed.

"Beltran too," I insisted, putting my teeth back to her neck.

"Yes, yes." Her voice was weak. "Beltran too." But her response had the timbre of a lie.

"Do not lie to me, Evedra." I grabbed her forearms and shook her. "What love is this you bear Beltran?"

She shook her head. "No love, Cruxim. I bear him no love."

"Liar." I brushed her neck with my lips, and the hollow at her throat quivered. "Tell me," I insisted. "The truth!"

"He was my brother."

I pushed her away and returned to the bed.

"Once. Millennia ago. Before he became my pimp." She looked no more than twenty-five, but, of course, that was deceptive.

I brushed my hair back from my face, suddenly ashamed of my treatment of her. She was my enemy, and I hated her, yet still I pitied her. "He made you ... this?"

She looked at the floor and then turned her dark eyes back to me. "It is better than what you would make me."

"What?" I did not understand.

"What you made Joslyn—a traitor to her own kind."

"Oh, Evedra," I said, and I could not keep the pity from my voice. "He already made you that. Millennia ago."

She fell silent for some seconds, thinking. "You love her," she said. "She is a Vampire and you, a Cruxim, yet you love her."

I gave her no answer but my silence.

"You love them both. How is it that you have not killed her?"

Growing weary of her already, I responded, "How is it I have not killed you?"

"I have never seen a Cruxim with so much control."

The comment piqued my interest. "Presumably, you have not known many Cruxim."

She turned her head to the side and studied me intently. "I am twelve hundred years old. I have met more than a hundred Cruxim. None has shown mercy. Few have even bothered with restraint. None have we been able to kill. It is only by luck, and with Beltran's protection, that I have escaped them."

"And what protection he offers," I said sardonically. "What a protective sibling he is! Tell me, do you get to keep a cut of your earnings, or does your brother take it all?"

"My brother takes whatever he wants," she said with a trace of bitterness as she smoothed down her skirt. "He always has." For a second, she looked almost mortal.

"He always will," I said. "Unless he is stopped."

"And I am to believe that you will stop him? You—out of all the Cruxim who have failed, who continue to fail—you will stop him? He knows now, Cruxim, about your weakness. What a valuable piece of information that was. And there are many thousands of us here." She shook her head. "No, Cruxim. You will not stop him."

I approached her again, calmly this time. "Then I have no use for you."

She put up her hands, still bound. "There is nothing you can do, Cruxim, to save me. I am damned."

"Yes," I agreed. "As is Joslyn. He damned you both. I cannot save you, Evedra." The words hung heavily on me. "But I can spare you."

"For the price of my brother."

"There is always a price, Evedra. Every prostitute knows that."

FOURTEEN

"Unbind me," Evedra pleaded before she set about telling me the information I required. "If I am to trust that you will spare me for this betrayal, you must trust me enough to remove these."

It sounded fair. Sitting her on the bed, I stood by the door and listened as she recounted the citadel's defenses, its access points, and the army of Vampires under Beltran's command who protected it. As she spoke, the enormity of my task became clear.

The citadel had been built to contain sixteen thousand people for a year-long siege, and there were thousands of Vampires within its walled enclosure. Ramparts that protected the citadel itself were equipped with guardhouses and cannon, and inside, dry ditches prevented a headlong attack on the solid, square citadel building. Even flying in would be almost impossible by day due to the cannon. By night, even if my approach were secretive, the bats would surely raise the alarm.

"I cannot think how you mean to do it, Cruxim," she warned me.

"We," I told her. "We mean to do it."

Satisfied that she was telling the truth, I bound her again and cut a strip of sheet to use as a gag. Of course, she protested, but trust or no, I was not fool enough to leave a Vampire, and especially one related to Beltran, alone and ungagged in a boarding house at dusk. I lit the lamp for her and took up the jar of whale oil.

"I am sorry," I whispered, before turning for the door. "Be safe here, and quiet. I will return within the hour."

Immediately, I made my way to the Eglise St Martin. The temperature had dropped with the sun, and the stone was cool against my skin as I alighted on the windowsill and pulled myself into the tower, hoping beyond hope that the Vampires who had slumbered there by day on my earlier visit still remained.

The room was emptier than before, but not by much. The room's inhabitants still slept, but the cage full of mortals had gone. I crept further in and, once certain they were asleep, I began my work.

The oil shone in the candlelight as I made runnels of it back toward the fire and poured it toward a pile of them who lay together in one darkened corner. Then I fluttered up to the rafters. The movement of my wings made a gentle hum in the room, but I tried to slow their flapping so I could hover before the dangling Vampires, my teeth bared.

The first made barely a whimper as I drank my fill of him. When, his life having flowed away, his body made to sink to the floor, I clutched him up and placed him down gently. Five Vampires I dispatched this way before those in the corner began to stir and I had to put the rest of my plan into fruition. Quickly, I flew to one more of the dangling creatures, hovering below him, my mouth at his throat. He wore a long cloak of burgundy velvet, which wrapped his cold body as his blood gushed into me and enlivened me. With one hand, I painted the cloak's hem and seams with the oil. He stirred and called out, as if awaking from a nightmare, and I took his last droplet of blood and let him plummet, lifeless, to the marble floor below. He landed close to the fire. His cape caught with a great whoosh of flame that licked along the oil on the floor to catch at the clothes of the Vampires in the corner. Soon, the flames also ignited the heavy drapes. Smoke curled upwards into the rafters, where it coiled among the beasts that dangled there. Screeching and screaming as the blast of heat hit them, they dropped like bees stunned by the apiarist's smoker. I snatched one up greedily, and then another. Everywhere Vampires rushed for the exit. I flew among them like the angel of death. Most failed to notice me in their haste to avoid the flames. Each pushed others out of the way in the rush to the windows. Only one seemed to notice me among them.

"Cruxim!" it screamed in a high, unnatural voice more piercing than a falsetto. "Cruxim. Catch him!"

But the others were too concerned with evading the flames to pay him any notice, and I quickly ended his commands with my teeth in his neck. The bloodlust made me impervious to the cinders and smoke until I felt the rasp of my lungs and sought the exit myself.

Outside, gray smoke billowed from the church and Vampires spewed from the exits out into the dark of early evening. Some of them hurried to transform themselves into bats, but I flung myself upon them. Five, ten, fifteen … thirty—even I could not say how many I consumed, but I caught them then in terror. I swooped down on them as they fled, blacked with soot and fearful in the darkness, and I carried them to Lucifer. Of course, more escaped me, and those who did not, set up such a great howling that every Vampire in St Martin de Re had to know of the inferno. They rolled on the ground, slapping at their hair and clothes and screaming. And with each scream, more appeared. Like a thunderstorm that darkened the horizon over the Breton Strait, they massed in the air above the citadel. Seeing their approach, I dropped to the ground and hid my wings. I pulled my hat down low and hurried for the side street just as the foul wind of their wings battered the church, sending the cinders scattering.

Without looking back, I rushed back to Madame Bourret's boarding house.

Evedra was sitting up. She had obviously been listening at the door, as when I'd turned the key I had heard her scurrying away. She had worked the gag down, and I wondered whether she had screamed out in my absence. If she had, it seemed no one in Madame Bourret's boarding house had paid any mind to a prostitute bellowing in the room of a wealthy man, which attested to the character of my new residence.

"I am hungry," were the first words out of her mouth. "I must feed."

She looked paler than usual and her lips were blue and drawn.

"Very well. I have a task for you." I untied her and helped her to her feet. "Undress."

She looked at me skeptically.

"Undress," I instructed again as I unbuttoned my shirt.

"I will not fuck you, Cruxim." She sounded incredulous. "No matter the price."

I laughed at that. It felt good to laugh; it seemed an age since I had been amused. "Just undress." I unbuckled my trousers and slid out of them.

With some hesitation, she turned her back to me and said, "I need help."

I moved her silky blonde hair off her neck, trying to ignore the blue vein that marred her skin's ivory smoothness, and set about unfastening her corset. The buttons on her brocade bodice were tiny, her outfit expensive. She had a slim little waist above those shapely hips, and I wondered momentarily whether all of this might be in vain.

When her dress hung unbuttoned, I turned away again, not wishing to be further drawn by her blood or the voluptuousness of her bosom.

Naked, I moved to the washbasin and cleansed my face of soot. I wet my hair, smoothing it back and plaiting it into a braid at the nape of my neck. I could feel her eyes upon me, assessing my naked body. Vampire she was, but she was all whore, and I knew what she expected. Had I been a mortal, I would almost have hated to disappoint her.

I turned suddenly and caught her in her appraisal of me. Evedra blushed and covered her breasts with her hands. Looking down, she fumbled with her pantaloons.

"Leave those on," I instructed. "Here." I picked up my trousers from the floor and threw them at her, followed by my shirt.

"What?"

"Put them on. Over the top."

Her eyes remained upon me as I strode to the bed, where she had carefully laid out her bodice and petticoats.

Laughter burst from her when I put a leg into the first petticoat. "I never pegged you for a pervert, Cruxim. But, very well, let's play dress ups."

"Shhh," I cautioned. "Now you must help me with these infernal buttons." I shrugged into the bodice. The top of it bit into the underside of my wings, and it was too small: only the lowest buttons would fasten.

She laughed again as she attempted to pull it tighter around my waist, and then she ran her hands gently over my shoulders, over my wings. "Sir, I fear you're too big," she said provocatively. It seemed a well-practised lie.

"Far, far too big." She slid a hand around my waist, headed for my groin. Her touch, cold as it was, made me hungry; I stepped away from it abruptly, and she remembered who I was. What I was.

"Evedra, spare me your flattery and hand me your cape and bonnet." Once I had fastened the cape over the top, the mirror beckoned. The cape hid the half-buttoned corset and absence of breasts. I was thankful I had never been possessed of abundant body hair and my face, although masculine at the jaw, was passably pretty under the bonnet.

"Lovely." Evedra giggled again. "Angelic almost. How much should we charge for you by the hour?"

I smiled and tightened the bonnet. With a feigned curtsy, I reached out for her hand and drew her to the nightstand.

She giggled again, still expecting I know not what as I sat her on the bed and reached out to snuff the lamp. After a moment, when our eyes had adjusted to the darkness, I took the wick and rubbed it between my fingers until they blackened. Then I knelt before her and darkened her jaw and upper lip. With the hat on and the mannish clothes, she might pass as a man long enough to accomplish her task. My transformation seemed more convincing.

"Come." I pulled her up and showed Evedra her reflection in the mirror. She grimaced slightly.

"It will do. Let us visit your old hunting grounds."

Bats still circled above the city as we hurried to the center of town, where several girls were already on the street, selling their wares in the same alley where I had found Evedra.

"I will wait here." I leaned against a wall, my chin tucked into my non-existent bosom, trying to look inconspicuous in a street full of women who were anything but demure. "Make sure you find a big one. I wouldn't mind swapping this corset," I whispered. "And don't try to go anywhere. I am right here, watching."

The thought seemed to amuse her. Then she turned and walked up the street a distance to where a solidly built older woman had hitched her red skirt up to the thigh.

"Come on, lad," she coaxed. "Ol' Mathilde gives a discount to young boys. Let a real woman show you how it's done."

I saw Evedra nod and fumble in the pocket of her trousers as she stepped forward and took Mathilde's hand. Turning, she led the woman back down the street toward me.

Guilt and revulsion assailed me when I saw how willingly Mathilde wobbled to her doom. As Evedra embraced her, I turned away. It was only when I heard the thump of the prostitute's heavy body hitting the cobbles that I turned again. Evedra's eyes shone, and her lips and cheek were flushed scarlet with blood as she helped me drag the poor woman's body into the alley. I wondered, briefly, if Mathilde had children, but stopped myself. Might be her sacrifice would rid this town of Evedra and all her kind. Evedra. I looked at her, and more shame flooded me. Had I lied to her? Would I truly let her live? Even I could not say.

She smiled at me as she unfastened Mathilde's corset. "Now, give me my clothes back." She kept her eyes on me as we changed.

"What have you done?" Evedra asked as we left the alley and the plume of smoke from the Eglise could be seen obscuring the night sky. Prostitutes aside, the streets were quiet. No doubt the squeal of bats had alerted the citizens that it was a night best spent behind locked doors.

"I visited the church." I followed her in the direction of the citadel.

"Ah, clever. A diversion to draw some of them away from the citadel. They shall seek you even more now."

"Yes, but in my place they shall find a newborn Vampire named Elynne, your newest consort." I pursed my lips at her.

Evedra shook her head. "Mayhaps you lie to me, Cruxim. Or mayhaps I lied to you. What then would you call this bargain that we have?"

"I would call it false, Evedra, but only time will tell whether we honor our promises."

We turned a corner and the star-shaped ramparts of the citadel came into view at the alley's end. Bats stung the sky above and Vampires could be seen crowding beyond the gates.

"Do you have a sibling, Cruxim?" she asked, her eyes on the sky.

"Yes. One."

"A sister?"

"Yes."

"Would you kill her?"

"What need?"

"If you had need, would you kill her?"

"I have never known her; may never know her. She would not vex me so."

She paused and wrenched her eyes from the sky to my face. "And Beltran has known me," she said in a whisper and looked down at the cobbles. "You would not kill your sibling; yet you expect me to kill mine. Whatever he is—rapist, monster, torturer—he is my brother."

Already she was having regrets. I pitied her. "I do not expect you to kill him," I said, stepping ahead of her in my haste to reach the walled fortress. "I expect you to let me do that for you."

"You make it sound like a gift."

I raised my eyebrows in reply and noticed that crimson tears welled in the corners of her eyes.

Sometime later, when we drew close enough to be just out of earshot of the gatehouses, I stopped and pulled her into the shadows. "Evedra, I have been cruel to you." I wiped at a smear of charcoal that marred her cheek. "I cannot spare Beltran, but if you help me save Joslyn and Sabine, I will spare you. I promise you."

She huffed, and we strode on, our skirts swishing against the stone. "You walk like a man," she told me, unable to keep the irritation from her tone. "Perhaps you also lie like one."

"I have never been a man." I kept my eyes on the gatehouse. "I would not know."

"Who goes there?" called a sentry when we reached the outer ramparts near a guardhouse.

"Castellan, it is but I." Evedra stepped into the dim light thrown by candelabra on the walls. She took my hand. "And my friend—Elynne."

"Come forward more, where I can see you." The sentry, an elderly Vampire with steel-gray hair and eyes, raised a flaming torch.

I followed Evedra into the light, conscious to keep my eyes down and my face concealed by the bonnet and by shadow.

"She is newly born." Evedra covered for me.

"Aye, she still has the look of a mortal about her," the guard said, staring at me. "That must be it. You have good taste, Evedra. I wouldn't mind a go of her myself."

"Quiet!" Evedra shot him a look that silenced him even more than her command. "She is for my brother."

Castellan chuckled. "Must Beltran get all the beauties? Or are you replacing that bitch Joslyn?" He lowered his voice to a whisper. "Say what he will, she has wounded him sorely this time. There is such a fine line between love and hate. But something tells me you know that, Evedra."

She sneered at him but said nothing.

"You best hurry," Castellan told her. "There's a Cruxim abroad. They say he set fire to the Eglise, killed more than thirty while they slept, and burned twelve more. Beltran is livid and set to wreak his vengeance."

"How can my brother hurt a Cruxim, unless you mean to torture his traitorous bitch?"

"Might be that is exactly what I mean, and the lioness too. If their screams won't draw a Cruxim out, what will?"

"He will come," Evedra said, her voice hard. "I promise."

"Then it seems it will be quite a show."

The guard creaked open the heavy gates, and Evedra took my hand and led me in. The sentry's eyes followed me as I passed.

Inside, Vampires thronged the walled, torch-lit walkways to the main citadel. Evedra dropped my hand; my palms were sweating.

How did I hope to get out of this hell alive?

Vampires nodded at Evedra as she passed, but I kept my eyes down and my mouth shut.

"Don't worry," she whispered. "Beltran has been making so many newborns that no one will know any different."

But I did. My skin crawled with the proximity of so many enemies, and my wings ached for release from under the cape. I willed my wings to stay flat, my fangs to remain hidden, and tried to move more gracefully. When we reached the marble steps of the citadel, the crowd parted to let Evedra through.

"Where is my brother?" she demanded as we climbed the staircase. "I have something for him."

It suddenly dawned on me how amused they would all be if she turned me over to him. A Cruxim in petticoats, defenseless in the midst of so many foes. Already I could hear howls and jeers coming from a room to the right.

As we entered the throng, she pulled me to one wall and pushed me up against it, as if to kiss me. Leaning in close, so close that the scent of her blood filled my nostrils and her breath tickled my ear, she said, "Stay here, and say nothing. I have made my part of the bargain. You are here. What you do now is upon you."

I nodded, and she kissed my cheek. Leaving me, she pushed through the crowd. The air was rank with the stale, metallic smell of blood, and the room was hot. I cursed the cape and skirts and wondered how women wore them. To my left was a window with a stone step beneath. I made my way over to it, inching through the crowd until I could pull myself onto the step for some fresh air and a better view.

"Ah, Sister is that you?" By the opposite window Beltran stood, holding out his hands as Evedra approached. A large box of sturdy oak, the top an open crosswork of iron bars, sat to his right. Next to it was a stone table, stained red-black and encrusted with blood. Unwashed instruments were discarded around it, and a bucket beneath was filled with a thick, dark liquid. I noticed something dangling from one end of the table. My guts twisted when I realized what it was: Sabine's tail.

Turning to the window with an involuntary shudder, I struggled to keep my face a mask of apathy. My poor Sabine. I had never known one so strong, so fierce or proud, but how much torture could she bear? I wondered how many of the foul beasts I could I kill if I went in now? Too few, was the answer.

"Evedra." Beltran took his sister in his arms and kissed her full on the mouth. "You taste of char," he complained and pulled back.

"Yes, the sky outside is full of ash. Someone set fire to the Eglise St Martin."

Beltran's eyes narrowed. "Yes. Someone. We are still dousing the flames. Sybil and Montagnon writhe in the infirmary and will carry their scars for eternity, and we are more than three scores fewer than at sunset. But no matter, Sister. We will find the Cruxim, and we will bury him."

"How so, Brother? He is immortal."

Beltran cackled. "Ah, yes. Immortality. What a shocking lie it is." The room erupted into a fragile laughter.

"Evedra, we are immortal."

"Until he finds us."

"Silence! What feeds us, Sister, but mortals?"

"Nothing. Nothing feeds us but blood and lust."

Beltran laughed. "Yes, well blood feeds him too, but not mortal blood."

The crowd brayed.

"You are certain of this? How do you know mortal blood is his weakness?"

Beltran's voice grew quiet. "Do you mock me, Sister? Do you doubt me?"

"No, Brother." She put a hand on his arm. "But we must be sure."

"Yes." Beltran calmed a little.

"Did you make good coin last night, dear Sister? You look exhausted." He ran one hand down her body and put out the other, as if expecting her to drop gold into it.

Evedra shook her head. "I was busy."

"Busy!" Beltran's slap came out of nowhere. "Busy fucking. You always did like that too much." I noticed his eyes narrow jealously. "What about jewels? Gold? Silver? Surely you have something to add to our pile."

He gestured to a mound of metal: coins and jewelry, gold, silver, bronze, and lead heaped nearby. The Vampires were stockpiling their wealth. I wondered what for.

My eyes moved from the gold around the dimness of the rest of the room. In a far dark corner, I could make out a cage.

In it sat Sabine.

They had bound her feet and she was slumped against the cold bars, her head hanging limply. I could see from her color that she had not eaten. Vampires encircled her cage, all jeering and mocking her, and near the door stood two men, mortal it seemed, both stout and well muscled and bearing swords.

"What is it for?" Evedra asked, moving to the pile of metal.

"You will see, Little Sister. You will see."

He put out a hand, clicking to two Vampires who stood behind him. At his command, they picked up something off the floor and turned. I glimpsed a flash of brown leg. Then my heart leaped as I saw who they held.

Joslyn was bound and gagged but otherwise naked. The men slit her feet bindings with a sword and stood her up before Beltran. I could see no wounds upon her, although one fine cheekbone was red and bruised. The crowd booed and sneered.

"Silence," Beltran bellowed. "Come." He put out a hand to Joslyn.

Her legs were weak, and the guard pushed her a little as she stumbled towards him.

"See, Sister." He turned back to Evedra. "We have two secret weapons."

He took Joslyn's face in his hands and kissed her deeply. It was painful to watch. I turned away.

"Say you love me, Little Dove," he cooed.

Joslyn nodded.

"Oh, do not nod, Joslyn!" He led her to the stone table, and picking her up as if she weighed nothing, placed her upon it. "Say it. Say the words themselves, so I can glean the truth of them. So many lies, Joslyn. So many lies you have told me. And even more lies you told the doctor, I hear. What are we to believe?"

"I love you," she said.

It was a good lie, but a lie nevertheless.

"Beltran," she said with more urgency, "I love you. I came back for you."

"For me, you say? Or for him?"

"For you. Oh, Beltran, for you. I was wrong, so wrong. How could I love a thing like that?" She shuddered.

More theatrics.

Beltran pushed her head back and gazed intently into her eyes, searching for the truth. She leaned up to him and her lips sought his.

"She's a lying bitch." A man stepped from the shadows. Gandler—although no longer wizened and stooped with age. "Kill her, Beltran. Gut her. She betrayed you, and she lied to me. She cannot be trusted."

"No," Beltran said, and then he turned to Joslyn. "But you are good at betrayal, aren't you, Little Dove?"

Joslyn shook her head. "I was confused."

"Then let me say this clearly." He stroked a finger down her bruised cheekbone and then forced her roughly down onto the table.

"I will forgive you. How could I not forgive you? I made you this." His finger traced her lips, her neck, her shoulder, her breast. "Do you remember? Of course you do."

Someone in the crowd whistled as Beltran unbuckled his belt and forced himself into her, his hands gripping her wrists.

Joslyn! I moved as if to rush to her, and then I noticed Evedra, too, turn away. Her eyes searched the crowd for mine, and she shook her head.

But it was too much for me to bear. I leaped off the window and pushed my way to the front of the crowd.

"Curious, are you lovely? I could show you how to do that if you like." I felt a man's hands grabbing at my buttocks and turned briefly to see the sentry, Castellan, leering at me. Ignoring him, I pressed on to the front, trying desperately to control the molten fury that roiled inside me.

Joslyn moaned, and still playing her role, tried to kiss him again. But Beltran pulled his lips away from her and thrust harder.

"I will forgive you only if you will do one thing for me." He nodded to Gandler, who came forward and took one of her hands, binding it to the table. "Only if you will betray him like you betrayed me, like you betrayed Dr. Gandler here. Turn him over to me, and I will let you live. Should you refuse? The daylight take you." He thrust harder, but there was no passion in it, only power.

"Of course. He means nothing to me," Joslyn said and clutched at Beltran again with her free hand, but he shook her hand away and climbed off her.

"Do not do this, Beltran," Joslyn cried as Gandler took her other hand and tied it down too. "He did not want me. He never wanted me," Joslyn cried.

For the first time in her act, I saw the truth. The scars I had given her.

"I hate him. I would gladly see his end," she said. And then the slight blink of another lie.

"Good." Beltran smiled. "Then tell us where he is."

"He is ... he is not here," she said. "I left him in Provins."

"Liar!" Gandler bared his fangs viciously and climbed up on the table. "These are lies, all lies." He brandished a sharpened razor.

"You lie to me, Joslyn. I am disappointed. You see, we know he is here." Beltran buttoned his trousers and cinched the belt. "Did you lie, too, about the mortal blood? About it killing him?"

"I ... I. No. I love you, Beltran," she whimpered.

"Such a beautiful face." Gandler knelt over her.

"Beltran, get him off me," Joslyn screamed. "Beltran!"

It is now, I thought. *It must be now. This is more than I can bear. But Sabine...*

Gandler made a shallow slice down Joslyn's cheek. "How that Cruxim must have loved this beautiful face."

A cacophony of shrieks rang from the assembly of Vampires.

"Bring out the cat, too," Beltran called. The crowd parted and four Vampires entered, each holding one of Sabine's paws. Her head lolled as they hefted her toward the table.

It was all I could do to keep from calling out at the sight of her.

She had clearly been given some stupefacient, as her green eyes were open, her feline tongue protruding slightly. With a heave, they slung her up onto the table, the opposite end to Joslyn. Sabine made a soft mewling as her head hit the stone. Her wings, I noticed, had been sawn off.

I put my hand to my mouth, forcing myself not to bellow in anguish. How would we ever escape here now?

"Let her, too, see what happens to those who love him." Beltran laughed. "You see, she is lucky. Each day she is renewed, born again ... but you ... well, my pretty Joslyn, how would he like you with a scar?"

"He does not like me now, Beltran. Please, please let me stay beautiful for you."

Sabine struggled on the table, the pain jolting her out of her sedation. It was as I thought: Gandler would not want her unconscious for long. She growled.

"These breasts," Gandler moved to Sabine and slid the scalpel from her face down her chest, leaving a thin strip of red where his hand had passed.

I heard Sabine's feline scream of pain and rage.

"So full and yet so pert. So human—for a cat." Gandler cupped one in his hand and lifted the scalpel to cut it. "He must have loved these, too. Shall I cut one off? We can feed it to him when he comes."

"No." Joslyn struggled against her bindings. "No."

"See, Joslyn, this could be you. Do you want to spare the lioness her pain? Or spare yourself? Tell us where he is, and all of this could be over." Blood began to drip from the table edge as Gandler held up his bloody trophy to the triumphant braying of the crowd.

"Do not." Sabine's voice was low and broken. "Joslyn, do not tell. They will kill him."

"He is coming for you, Sabine. He is coming to save you. He loves you," Joslyn said, her words a rush.

"Nooooo!" I hurtled forward to the table. "NO! I am coming for you both." Tearing at the cape that hindered my wings, I flew at Gandler, knocking the razor from his hand.

"To hell with you!" I screamed as the blade clattered to the table. I clutched it up and plunged it deep into his black heart. His blood washed over me and stained the table crimson, but I clamped down on the wound and sucked the life from him, discarding his shriveled corpse in an instant.

There was no time to crow over his death, over the satisfaction of finally removing such evil from this world. Pandemonium broke out. From everywhere, Vampires rushed at me, and I threw them off, slashing with the razor and biting indiscriminately. At one point, I thought Sabine was beside me, dripping blood and roaring as she tore out throats and dismembered limbs, but in the haze of my fury and bloodlust, I was unsure. The Vampires came at me in waves, one after the other. They had torn the bonnet and petticoats from me and tugged and bitten at my wings until bloodied feathers littered the floor. Male after female, I slew them.

I threw them from windows and impaled them with the razor, and all the while I drank others to their deaths. But still, somewhere in the frenzy, my mind knew there was one among them I was searching for above all others: Beltran.

Blood covered my face and hands, but whether it was mine or theirs, I knew not. Sweet blood filled my gullet and clouded my judgment, but still vengeance went hungry. With colossal strength, I fought and fed until a familiar taste stopped me, and a startled face before me cried, "Stop, stop, Ame. Please, stop."

I released my hold on the girl's throat and pulled back.

It was Joslyn. In my fury, I had almost forgotten she was one of them. The sweetest of them.

Evedra! I had forgotten about her too. Had I killed her? I swung my head wildly and saw her behind me, fighting off another swarm of Vampires who were heading my way.

"Fly!" she yelled at me. "Take them now and fly, or you will die here, Cruxim."

But I could not.

"Where is your brother?" I roared at her. "Where is Beltran?"

Leaving Sabine and Joslyn, I tried to fly upward on my broken, torn wings and spied him rushing for the door, a contingent of bodyguards with him.

Evedra shook her head. "Leave," she said. "Leave now! There are more coming."

"Coward! Come and face me," I screamed. I swung my head like a berserker. Shaking off several more Vampires who tore at my arms and chest and face with their teeth, I thundered towards him.

"Cruxim." Beltran turned. Gesturing to his bodyguards, he said, "Bind him."

Still I half-flapped, half-ran to him. Spurred by fury, I tore the bodyguards limb from limb until I reached Beltran and spun him around to face me.

"Have you come to meet your death?" he goaded, and then punched me in the mouth.

"No, I have brought you yours." I wrenched his head back so forcefully his neck near snapped. Ignoring a new wave of undead that clambered over my back, I bared my teeth, preparing to sink them into his throat. A choking sensation stopped me.

"Bite me then," Beltran said as he tugged at the silver chain of Danette's that hung around my neck. His hand sizzled as he gripped it, but he pulled it tighter until it choked into my flesh. "Everyone you ever loved remains lost to you. Joslyn will still go to hell."

"You go to hell!" I spluttered, letting go of his throat with one hand to reach up and break the chain. He struggled free and stepped back, right as a heavy weight crashed into the back of my skull. A lead bar clattered to the ground, and I staggered for a second then made to step toward him again.

A wisp of smoke curled up from his hand where he clutched the silver crucifix. Turning it, he plunged the longest end straight toward my heart.

"No!" The sound was disjointed, disconnected by the sizzle of flesh as someone stepped in front of me. "No."

A body fluttered to the ground before me, a naked woman, her blue eyes enormous with mortality.

"Joslyn! No!" I fell to my knees and wrenched the searing silver cross from her breast. Blood followed, thick and sluggish as honey.

"Why did you do this? Why? This would have been but a wound to me!"

She gasped. Her eyes met mine, and her lips moved in a silent kiss.

"Do not leave me, Joslyn," I begged. I kissed her lips. Her eyes. "Joslyn!" I said again, but already the color had flooded from her face.

She opened her mouth and then closed it again. And then, she was gone.

FIFTEEN

"Wake him." The voice pounded in my head. "I said: wake him. I want him to see this."

It was Beltran's voice, and that alone made me want to close my eyes and never open them again. He still lived. Joslyn died. And he still lived. My heart felt dead in my chest, my body a hollow vessel jogged upon waves of nausea and guilt. *Joslyn is dead,* I thought. *And perhaps Sabine too. And he lives. And I live.* Even hatred felt futile.

"Wake up!" A hand slapped my face. "Wake up. We have a surprise for you."

I opened one eye. Vampires: a horde of them. I sighed and tried to move my legs but could not. Opening both eyes, I found myself strapped to a wall, my wrists and ankles fastened with thick, buckled leather. Beyond, the sea churned purple and green. I was on a boat.

"Why have you not killed me already?" I asked no one in particular.

"I wanted you to see this first, Cruxim."

"See what? Your death?" I stared at him, loathing my

only weapon.

Beltran laughed. "Oh, Cruxim! Always so optimistic. Look at you." He gestured to my restraints. "Trussed up in the middle of the Caribbean and still threatening death to me." He sat down on the deck before me, relaxed, cocky as ever, and chuckled. "Tell me, where is Sabine?"

I glowered at him.

"It is not a riddle, Cruxim." He grinned. "Where do you think she is? Let me see. She had no wings. She had no teeth." He checked them off on his fingers. "She had no tail. She had no help, thanks to you. Do you think she escaped after you were taken? Or do you think she fought for you, just like Joslyn did—or tried to? Oh, I am sure she would have given her life for you, too. And yet … here you are … still alive, while they are…"

I remained mute; rancor choked a rebuttal in my throat.

"I don't know what it is about you…" He paced before the wall, inspecting me. "What makes women love you so? Sabine would do anything for you. Anything. Joslyn gave her life for you." A scowl made his handsome face quite ugly. "You even bewitched my own sister, it seems."

He stood, and his voice dropped to a whisper. "You made me kill Joslyn. I loved her. And you made me kill Evedra," he snarled. "I loved her too."

"You never loved either." I spat on the deck. "You never loved."

"And you did? Tell me, Cruxim, which did you love: Joslyn or Sabine?"

"Both."

He laughed again. "Both. As if Joslyn were not enough. As if Sabine were not enough for you!"

His words came at me like a blow to the face.

"Did you ever wonder how that made them feel? Both vying for you. Both fighting for you. Both dying for you, even. Well, which did you love more?"

I looked away, out to sea. Every molecule of me wept for them, but some part of me knew he was right. I had failed them—both of them. They had loved me too well. They had both loved me more.

Beltran strode up to me and clutched my hair in his hands. He turned my head to where a solid object, covered by a cloak, sat on the deck. "Look at what your greed has left you. Your precious pride, your righteousness." He turned to the group of Vampires behind him. "Show him."

One of them strode forward and pulled off the cloak.

"One killed by silver; the other, gold!" Beltran hissed triumphantly.

A perfect golden replica of Sabine stood before me, her haunches bunched as if to leap, her mouth open to bite, tail held high, both perfect breasts pert, one arm raised as if to strike.

"Sabine!" I cried. "What have you done to her?" I struggled against my bonds. "Sabine."

"Only what we had planned before you ruined our little party in your petticoats." He smiled and stroked the golden figurine's head. "I much prefer gold, don't you, to limestone? It took a while to boil it all up, of course, so we had to wait until the next evening." He walked around the figure, stroking it. "But I think it is better that she has her wings, and her breasts. My statuette looks so much more impressive that way." His hand slid over the smoothness of her breasts and moved up to the golden-feathered wings. "Of course, we had to chip away the excess once we poured the boiling metal into her cage, but it was worth it, don't you think? Such a likeness."

I screamed out in anguish and tugged at the restraints again, but they did not budge.

"Oh, Gandler was desperate to find her anchorstone and destroy Sabine forever, but I think this is much nicer. It's an alloy, of course. Mostly lead, a little gold, some silver. Heavy as a stone. It should sink just as nicely. I considered keeping it in my chamber, but Sphinxes are such contrary creatures, I doubt I would ever quite trust her."

I grimaced. *Sabine, what have they done to you, my love? What have they done? By night locked in stone, by day in gold at the bottom of the ocean.*

I remembered her words, *eternity in a cage,* and I sobbed openly.

Beltran rolled his eyes. "Are you a man or an immortal? Do not weep, for heaven's sake. I cannot abide weeping. Shall I put your petticoats back on?"

"I will kill you!"

"Do you hear it?" he asked the others. "He says he will kill me—again." He chuckled and slapped one thigh. "That never gets tired."

Once more I tried to free myself from the restraints.

"She is not dead," I spat.

"No. One day, when I find her anchorstone, perhaps she will be delivered to eternity, but until then, no. Think of her as just asleep, Cruxim. A very long, very cold sleep. Such a shame cats just hate water." He gestured to the three strongest-looking Vampires who came forward and attached chains to the statuette. Passing them through a pulley system, they hauled the statue into the air and swung it over the side of the ship's prow.

"I wanted you to see this ... before we killed you." Beltran smirked. "Thanks to Sabine and Joslyn, we know how to do that now. I had long suspected it, you know, but to have it confirmed ... well. It has been fun, Cruxim, but it will be such a relief to have you gone." He wiped his hands one over the other theatrically and flicked them towards the ocean. Then he said, "The cabin boy."

Another Vampire came forward, pushing before him a boy of about fourteen whose arms were crusted with scabs.

"Now, drink, Cruxim. Won't it be sweet, the oblivion of it

all? Put an end to it. You have lost Joslyn. Lost Sabine. What else is there to live for anyway?"

"There is my purpose."

Beltran rolled his eyes again. "Your purpose? Ah, yes. To destroy us all, or some such." He let out a long sigh. "You have failed at this purpose, Cruxim, countless times. You are outnumbered, outgunned. You will fail at your mission again and again, and all for what? Do you even know? Does your God whisper to you? Does he tell you that you are so different from us? We eat them..." He thrust the cabin boy forward. "You eat us. Just as the lion eats the gazelle, or the fox eats the hare. Yet still you think yourself so much better than us. So far above us. So goddamn arrogant. So holy." He spat on the deck and pushed the cabin boy to his knees before me. "Now, drink!"

I shook my head. "I will not."

"Drink!" Beltran kicked the boy closer.

"No."

"DRINK!" Beltran rushed at the child and scooped him up, pushing the boy's face up against me, his neck to my lips.

"I will not!" I raged.

"Very well." Beltran dropped the boy at my feet. "Montagnon, the syringe."

A green-eyed Vampire whose face was taut with burns left the deck and returned a moment later from the cabin. He carried a glass syringe like the one Joslyn had used to dispense her blood to me in doses.

Remembering her sacrifice made me crave death. *And it is death approaching*, I thought. I glanced over at the golden statue of Sabine, still dangling above the water. *Death take me, but send me to hell, for all of my loves are there.*

Bending over the weeping child, Beltran calmed him. "Now, now, we shall only need a little, Benjamin, I should think. Here, give me your arm."

I watched as he slid the syringe in and drew out a full vial.

"There's a good boy," he soothed. "Montagnon, take him away."

I fixed my eyes on Sabine's figurine, on her once-green eyes, now gold but still dispensing fury. Even when I heard Beltran approaching, I refused to turn away from her.

"Let her drop," said Beltran, and I felt the cold steel of the needle against my vein as the Vampires released the chains that held the golden idol of my love. As she plummeted into the waves, I heard Beltran whisper, "Goodbye, Cruxim."

Sixteen

The sea heaved beneath a curdled sky as the first trickle of the boy's blood mingled with mine. It felt like a punch, followed by a swoon—so harshly smooth it was. I cried out, unable to control my reaction, and then I felt it surging through my body, filling me, healing me. Exulting me.

It is sweeter even than Joslyn's, I thought in wonder. It was sweet, and good, and carefree, and innocent. Every molecule that filled me felt alive with emotion. And in the song of the boy's blood, I finally heard my Maker.

Like a drug, the blood coursed through me, rushing to my head and to my heart. When I felt its itch in every vein, I knew that Joslyn had lied to them. This was not death to me: it was death to those who enjoyed this sweetness daily, who robbed others of it willingly. In an instant, I knew why I hunted them: only to keep me from doing this! For centuries I had killed them, taking what passion and pleasure I could in the feel of their throats in my mouth, their blood-beat in my ears. But all the while, I dined on their hatred while they dined directly on soul.

Suddenly, I was ashamed, more ashamed than I had ever been. Each little death, my longing for Danette, for Joslyn, was nothing compared to this need. Oh, how I pitied the boy and all humankind. And how I hated Beltran for taking advantage of what I could not ... yet I knew that hatred was futile in the face of faith. It was as if I stood again amid the ruins of that castle outside Barcelona, watching him defile my dreams for Joslyn. But this time, I blamed not him nor Joslyn, but something greater than all of us.

How is it fair, Lord? my mind cried. *How is it fair that my mouth is filled with their bitterness and sorrow, and yet these creatures have their glut of euphoria and immaculate purity?*

For the first time, His voice spoke directly to my heart: *Innocence is always fairer than wickedness, and more desirable. Their master deals in pleasures, and yours in absolutions. But yours will free you, and theirs will enslave them.*

Then help me, I cried. *I am alone. You never help me! You are never alone.*

A flood of power poured through me. Yes, Beltran had stolen Joslyn's innocence, just as he had taken the boy's and injected it into me. Clasping my hands into fists, I slammed them away from the wall that restrained me, tearing the leather straps out with a resounding crunch.

With a furious howl, I broke free and surged into the air, trailing chain and sections of the wall behind me.

Before me, Vampires slithered over the deck, their hands over their ears. For once, Beltran looked truly afraid of me. He scrabbled backward, out of my reach.

Ignoring him, I plunged over the side and into the bubbling, freezing ocean. My eyes open, seeking the glint of gold, I swam down and down and down until there was no breath left in me.

SEVENTEEN

Sand chafed at the corner of one eye and my dry, swollen tongue worried at a small shell that clung to my lip. The sea filled my mouth like the ferryman's coin, and I ached so much I wondered if I had not reached the Styx.

My head felt leaden, but I raised it and glanced around. Sand. Stitched together with beach morning glory and beaded with shells. Beyond me, the viridian waters of the Caribbean seemed to mock me with their stillness. I crawled to my knees. Thirst and pain forced me to settle there awhile, forehead to the sand, the throbbing in my brain unimaginable.

I remembered, then, that everything was lost. Sabine to the bottom of the ocean, to eternity in a golden cage. Joslyn to the fires of hell. And I felt more alone than I ever had.

You are never alone.

When I finally looked up, it was at the slim legs of someone standing over me.

The skin was pale and smooth as white marble, and for a moment, I cursed. *I cannot deal with another of them right now.* I stayed as I was, facedown on the sand, until I felt a gentle hand stroke my wings.

My wings!

Immediately, I spun over, flipping onto my back to conceal them. The sun shone through the silver hair of the woman who stood over me and illuminated the argent tips of her own wings. I put a hand up to my eyes to see her better.

Her eyes were as pale and shining as a waxing moon, and I recognized her even without the red cape.

"It is time," she said.

I rubbed at my salt-stung eyes. "Are you real? What are you?" I stammered, sure in my soul that I already knew the answer.

"I am real." She answered with a smile. "I am Cruxim."

AUTHOR'S NOTE

Thank you for reading Cruxim; I hope you enjoyed it. Amedeo, Sabine, and more of his mythological brethren will return in two more books in the DARK GUARDIAN series, Creche and Creed, revealing the truth about Amedeo and Sabine's origins and the ongoing battle between the undead and the guardians.

If you enjoyed the novel, please consider leaving a review on Goodreads, Amazon, Kobo, Apple, Barnes and Noble or wherever else you purchased a copy. I would very much appreciate your feedback. You can also join my mailing list at http://eepurl.com/vk_bP to be the first to hear about new releases and special offers.

You can follow me on twitter @Authorandeditor or at http://www.karincox.wordpress.com or on Facebook http://www.facebook.com/KarinCox.Author or email me at cruxim@hotmail.com. I would love to know your thoughts.

Also by This Author

Along with more than thirty works of children's fiction, non-fiction natural history, social history, and many ghostwritten works of creative non-fiction, Karin Cox is the author of:

Cruxim, a gothic paranormal romance;
Crèche, sequel to Cruxim;
Creed, the final installment in the Cruxim trilogy.
What the Sea Wants, a suspenseful, Australian contemporary new adult novel.
Cage Life, a collection of short stories;
Crows & Other Beasts, a collection of two short stories;
Hey, Little Sister, an illustrated children's picture book;
Pancakes on Sunday, an illustrated children's picture book; and,
Growth, a collection of Poetry.

Her essays also appear in the Indie Chicks Anthologies: *Memories of Mom and Dad*, and *Ms. Adventures in Travel.*She lives in Australia and writes while caring for her daughter—undoubtedly her most important and precious work.

PRAISE FOR CRECHE

"he author has such a way of writing that the words just flow on the page, and I soon found myself completely caught up in the story and the history of it all. It has a very descriptive nature, without being over the top, which allowed my imagination to just take over and easily picture the story. Everything indicates that a major battle is on the horizon, so I'm sure the rest of the saga is going to be full of action and I can't wait to read it."
CLAIRE TAYLOR

"If you haven't read the first book yet, and you are looking for a supernatural thriller series that has a little bit of romance, a little bit of violence, and a lot of action, I highly recommend you get Cruxim and Creche!" KATHY, LITERARY R&R

"I thoroughly enjoyed the first book in this series, and Creche does not disappoint. One of the things that makes this book satisfying is the historical accuracy. While it is (clearly) entirely fiction, where it does reference Ancient Greece or Latin translation, it is accurate. The story took some unexpected turns which kept me intrigued. It is very much a page-turner and I can't wait for the final instalment to arrive!" KATHLEEN LOMMEL

PRAISE FOR CREED

"These books by Ms Cox are so beautifully written. They contain a story that is unique, well-thought out, and quite engaging. I've read the entire series in three days because it is that good. I have enjoyed the fact that with most novels you can predict what happens next. Not with these characters. Thank you, Karin Cox for such a beautiful, engaging story. Please keep them coming and I will continue to be a huge fan!" NICOLE

"This book was awesome, if you haven't read this series you should. I was worried about how this book would end after the first two but I was pleasantly surprised. There are still all of the twists and turns and there are some sad endings too but the way Ame's life ended was great. I love the entire series, great writing." PENNY

"What a fantastic ending to my favorite dark fantasy series. I don't want to give away any spoilers, but there were plenty of surprises ... and the author told it all in a way that left me breathless. Bravo!" BORN TO READ BLOGGER.

PRAISE FOR CAGE LIFE

"It was so good I just couldn't put my Kindle away while watching. I'm an avid reader and if I read a few pages and it doesn't jolt me, I delete it, but this one was fantastic." OSCAR LAPLANTE

"Ms. Cox not only knows how to communicate a story well, the writes with skill. Her characters are easy to identify with. The narration is good and very smooth." KAREN DOERING, PARENT'S LITTLE BLACK BOOK

"One can write a novel that is good, maybe even excellent, but it can never equal the power of an equally good short story. Reading short stories is somewhat like being a miner. You dig through the rocks, perfectly good rocks. Many have value, some less so. But then you pick up a rock and it sparkles. It is a gem and you know you've found something special. Such a story is Still Life - a true gem." LARRY MARSHALL

Praise for CROWS & OTHER BEASTS

"These two short stories were amazing. They are dark, no doubt about it, but very well written and paced.

Both stories are about violence. The first is seen through the eyes of an old, decrepit woman. The writing is so good that I was fascinated in spite of myself.

At the end of the second story, I was so surprised that I had to go back to the beginning to see if I had missed something.

I will definitely be reading more work by this author." BIRDIE TRACY

ACKNOWLEDGMENTS

My sincerest thanks to Michele Perry and Cheryl Shireman, who acted as early readers and as sources of unending encouragement. Thanks also to Sarah Billington, who introduced me to a little program called Write or Die, which revolutionized my writing time, and to Tara West and Greg James for serving as insightful beta readers.

To Jessica Meigs, who weeded out my peccadilloes, I am extremely grateful. Thanks also to my secretive but wonderful online writing group, without their encouragement, humor, and support I am sure I would be quite insane. Thanks are also due to Paul Beely from Create Imaginations. To Athanasios Galanis for his advice, and to Christine DeMaio-Rice, whose cover with biceps featured on the first edition, and of course, to Eden Crane for this cover.

Lastly, my gratitude goes to my wonderful girlfriends, many of whom gave their opinions on sections of the story, the cover, and the characters. This book would not exist without their friendship, and my life would be so much poorer without them.

www.ingramcontent.com/pod-product-compliance
Lightning Source LLC
Chambersburg PA
CBHW031309120626
46554CB00001BA/346